# The Discovery of Honey

# The Discovery of Honey

TERRY GRIGGS

BIBLIOASIS
WINDSOR, ONTARIO

FIRST EDITION

*Library and Archives Canada Cataloguing in Publication*

Griggs, Terry, author
    The discovery of honey / Terry Griggs.

Short stories.
Issued in print and electronic formats.
ISBN 978-1-77196-149-3 (softcover).--ISBN 978-1-77196-150-9 (ebook)

    I. Title.

PS8563.R5365D58 2017        C813'.54        C2016-907968-6
                                            C2016-907969-4

Edited by Daniel Wells
Copy-edited by Allana Amlin
Typeset by Chris Andrechek
Cover designed by David Drummond

Published with the generous assistance of the Canada Council for the Arts and the Ontario Arts Council. Biblioasis also acknowledges the support of the Government of Canada through the Canada Book Fund and the Government of Ontario through the Ontario Book Publishing Tax Credit.

PRINTED AND BOUND IN CANADA

MIX
Paper from
responsible sources
FSC® C004071
www.fsc.org

ANCIENT FOREST ™
FRIENDLY

# Contents

# Contents

*For John Metcalf*

# The Discovery of Honey

My parents were married in a high wind that was conceived in the tropics and born in a jet stream. As it crawled up the coast, playing with flags and sailboats, teething on cliffs and peninsulas, it matured into a lusty and vigorous gale. A product of incompatible air currents—polar and equatorial, with a trace of African simoom ancestry—it blew like a bastard, sweeping suddenly into the orchard where the wedding ceremony was proceeding at a lazy, mid-August, sun-sodden pace. My mother had scarcely breathed her consent to the marriage contract, exhaling a nervous and wavering "I do," when this wind arrived unannounced and uninvited, twirled the bees in their hives, flung Billy Murphy's dress up over her head, and gobbled up my mother's faint wafer-thin words in a roar. My father, who had himself that *very* second agreed to the whole ball of marital wax, for better or for worse, turned to his bride in surprise and gagged as the wind socked her veil into his open mouth.

Though inaudible, Reverend Cowley struggled on with the service, his pronouncement that my parents were "man and wife," the real clincher in most ceremonies, whirled up unheeded into the sky and yoked two gulls that were surfing on the turbulence. Immature Spartans and Paula Reds began to rain down from the trees and pummel the wedding guests, also beset by their best clothes—suits and silks that billowed hideously or slapped smartly. A charge of gate-crashing goats arrived, escapees from a damaged pen, keen to mingle with the guests and check out the windfalls. The wind raked its long fingers through my mother's hair until her demure, tidily tucked chignon, clean as a comma, became a cursive writing in the air. The translation: *Exalted mess.* My father turned again to speak to his gorgon-headed wife and was felled by a falling branch. Her French lace veil wrenched free from his clamped teeth and tore off across the fields like a spirit called home.

My grandmother, Albertha Pinkham, stood in the storm's eye like a plum preserve in a glass jar. As she watched her airborne chickens scud past served like volleyballs, some spiked to the ground, she pursed her lips, thinking, *When you turn a church upside down and dump the contents of a wedding into your backyard, what do you expect?* Her daughter, soft in the head after having read too many bride magazines, had insisted on being married in a natural and idyllic setting. Which goes to show how much work *she* had ever done in the orchard. Everything had to be just-so, countless niggling details nailed into place, and now those details had risen, chaotic and dangerous, in a stinging blinding swarm.

A woman's hat whizzed by Albertha's nose. She wished her own would take a ride, a mother-of-the-bride, fruit-and-flower festooned, caricature of a hat.

"Why not sew on a couple of tarts," Uncle Clyde had suggested, "some fox heads, fuzzy dice." ("Dry up, Clyde.") Albertha had witnessed her share of weddings over the years, but this one surely took the cake. *Jumping Jesus*, she then remembered, *the cake!* and tore off to the rescue, a swirling eddy of purple chiffon.

The wedding photographer meanwhile took twenty-four exposures of Billy Murphy hopping around in her frothy, champagne-pink underwear. She was frantically trying to gain control of the dress that had enveloped the top half of her like a bud that refused to bloom. (Worse, the undies were lacy with nibbles, as they were the edible kind and Billy hadn't been able to resist sampling them.) Her face was flaming—a scarlet pistil sealed in a periwinkle prison—as she conjured up the next social column in the town paper... *and the maid of honour wore (wink, wink) an appetizer!* The edible undies had been intended as a joke, a private post-reception one for her boyfriend Douggie, and not some self-immolating farce dished out for everyone's consumption.

The photographer was more entranced than titillated. He had no idea that it was physiologically possible for legs to blush. He *had* planned on taking some candid shots and a few arty double-exposed ones, but this wedding was like a circus with people running every which way, dodging flying debris, slipping and skidding on apples, hurtling into one another, their faces contorted as they shouted into the wind. Fleeting moments simply streaked by, hell-bent, stripped of sentimentality, too elusive to be captured on film. Although he did get a picture of the ring boy punching some other kid on the head, one of the best man wiping a sticky goo off his face with the tail of his tux, the flower girl spinning and spinning like a dust devil, a woman dancing with a goat, and several shots of his own hair, the unsprung crest of which kept flopping over the lens.

Unfortunately, he ran out of film and failed to document the thrilling and, I'm told, totally unexpected moment that Cousin Tony leapt out of a tree and grabbed Mother. Tony was a shy, stammering boy from a long braided line of cousinage, so retiring he seemed at times to recede into the obscuring folds of his own shadow. Well, this *very* Tony wrapped his arms around Mother, clasping her in a passionate embrace, and planted a prolonged kiss animate with hunger on her astonished lips. In the taxonomy of kisses a beaut, a stunner, top of the line. Unleashed, our no longer paralytically timid cousin cut a surprisingly dashing figure, his shrinking-violet nature in full and healthy bloom as he sank his eager rooting hands deep into the bustle of Mother's gown.

A buzz of shock ran through the wedding party. An appalled murmur snaked among the guests like a lighted fuse until someone exploded with *Did you ever!?*

But their outrage fizzled quickly, extinguished by the blanketing force of the wind, a renewed trumpeting blast that shook the trees fiercely and slammed the sky into the ground. Everyone took to their heels and fled, and the bullying wind tore after them, pushing and shoving, hounding them, pounding their backs and breathing its warm blustering breath down their necks.

The wedding refugees assembled in the barn, dishevelled, shaken, some laughing and joking, already putting the wind into words, siphoning off and savouring their share of the adventure. In that hushed, hay-scented sanctuary the storming bucking wind was corralled into story and tamed, told over and over like an animal taught to perform tricks. What had raged unfettered outside was within tempered and turned into so much hot air.

The mood among the guests had grown more relaxed and carefree. The awkwardness and constraint they had felt in their Sunday clothes and cinched belts and beauty-parlour hair had, like many of the things attached to the wedding, blown away. Everybody was mussed and rumpled, mauled by the tempest, ties pulled askew, shirts untucked, stockings twisted. (Marg Petty's knees had burst like bald heads through her new pantyhose and she didn't give a damn.) The veneer had blown off the occasion, as had the last shred of magic that had clung tenaciously to the ceremony. The enchanting vision of married life that had floated momentarily above them in the honeyed light of the orchard had descended on the dissenting voice of the wind into a form more familiar and homely.

Uncle Clyde fondly recalled that fight he'd had with Auntie Viv on their first anniversary, the one where she hurled a slab of raw veal at him that caught him on the chin and wrapped around his face like a mask, and she said, "How d'ya like yer scallopini, Meathead?" And there she was, dear heart, stumbling through the barn door with her blonde wig shoved under one arm and apples skewered on the spikes of her high heels. Marriage in their hands, as in the wind's hands, had been a gloriously malleable, earthy, and surprising thing.

Casualties were counted, the most regrettable of which was the wedding lunch, the fancy squares, cookies, and crustless sandwiches so prettily arranged on decorated tables in the backyard, that the wind had scooped up and tossed high into the sky like confetti. A fundamentalist church group picnicking miles away were the beneficiaries. There they sat in mid-grace, motionless and open-mouthed, as a swiftly approaching cloud of canapés and dainties arrived, hovered briefly overhead, then hailed down on them and into their capacious laps. In truth, they were less astounded by the miraculous arrival of the food than at the Lord's choice of pinwheels, pink bread, and the heathen caper.

The wedding cake had also gone missing in action. Before Albertha could save it, her fabulous confection met in a head-on collision with Buckwheat, Clyde's skewbald horse, and exploded into a thousand irretrievable servings. Running berserk after being stung by a hornet, Buckwheat not only shattered the cake into a sugary blizzard, but puréed the Big Boy tomatoes in the garden and danced like Silver on the wedding presents, flattening the flatware and reducing the porcelain to a much finer gift.

Among the human injuries: one goose egg and a fat lip. The goose egg was balanced on my father's head, laid in the hairline inlet near his temple when that falling branch had clobbered him, and the fat lip belonged to Lyle Sizer. Young Bobby, the ring bearer, was responsible for that one. Excitement had already stretched Bobby's nerves to the limit when the wind had come streaking through the orchard to pluck at those taut nerves, and flick his stick-out ears, and ruffle that neatly slicked hair. Then Lyle had appeared, turfed out of a ditch it looked like, shaggy with burs and beggar's ticks and smelling of marsh gas. A burly kid, Lyle loomed over Bobby, his fleshy arm extended, and, with more delicacy than anyone imagined him capable of, he plucked the wedding ring off the satin pillow held in Bobby's trembling hands. He took it as though it were being served to him, a priceless sweet, a gilded crystal-rich candy… and then he crammed it in his mouth.

"For sure, it's a stumper," Bobby would marvel years later. "Lyle Sizer *ate* my aunt's wedding ring. Swallowed'er down in one big gulp and smiled like a pig afterwards." Bobby's older brothers had always advised him that a man should resort to violence only in extreme circumstances, and in Bobby's six years he had never met a circumstance more extreme than this. That smile got smeared the whole length of Lyle's face, which, to Bobby's dismay, only inflated it to one outsized with satisfaction.

"Don't fret," Mrs. Sizer said later to my mother in the barn, "we'll have that ring back to you in a day or two." She was so offhand about it, you'd think ring-swallowing some routine nuptial practice in the Sizer clan, some purifying intestinal ritual. Mother was too dazed by that point to care anyway. Everything else had gone wrong, so it hardly mattered that her precious ring was churning in the acidic spin cycle of Lyle Sizer's gut, or that she had reaped the first sizzling kiss of her married life from another man. Assuming that she *was* married. She gave my father a skeptical look, and said (her mouth a crushed, fiery smear), "Are we hitched, or what?"

"Shit, darlin'," was all Father could say. All he could say because he'd forgotten her name, a name that only hours before he had applied like a garnish to almost everything he said. Usually, if he could work Mother into a conversation, he did. She was the verbal stowaway in his talk of trucks and tractor engines and outboards. His tongue had made love to every syllable of her delectable long-limbed name that now escaped him, that had slipped behind a concealing screen, that had withdrawn into a befuddling darkness, and he couldn't for the life of him see *who* she was.

Reverend Cowley walked up to them, a congratulatory hand extended to Father. "Morrie," he said, "you hit the ground flatter than pee on a plate. You all right?"

Father motioned him closer and asked, nodding in Mother's direction, "What's her name again?"

"Hah!" the Reverend barked, and flung his arm around father's shoulder. "Why, I guess it's music to your ears, son. Let me introduce you to *Mrs.* Morland Young."

Mother, gazing hellward, noticed that she was missing a shoe, that the ripped hem of her dress was filthy from dragging in the dirt, and that her train had split up the centre like a forked tongue. Her husband, she also noticed, was adorned with an obscene red knob on his forehead and an incredibly stupid expression on his face. A goat trotted up, Albertha's flamboyant, half-eaten hat in its mouth, and stared at her, golden-eyed and lubricious. She felt a slithering motion in her stomach, as though her innocent prenuptial butterflies had metamorphosed into something reptilian and poisonous. She wondered vaguely if she were going to throw up. A distinct possibility, and she could picture it, a barf bouquet cascading down the front of her dress and spilling onto her one white shoe. Ever since she'd been born, it seemed, people had been telling her that this was going to be her *Big Day*. And she believed them. But she'd had no idea that it was going to be *this* big, monstrous, like King Kong on the rampage and her captive in its huge, hairy paw. She stood there thinking of all the preparation and plans, the bone-wearying work, the sleepless nights that had been funnelled into the rapacious maw of this one culminating event in her life, and of just how it had turned on her with sharp teeth and—more disturbing—soft lips.

Outside, the wind continued to howl fortissimo, a robust love song, a manic lullaby that rocked the barn with a mad tempo. In the dusty animal-fragrant gloom within, silver flasks and mickeys began to appear out of dainty purses and suit pockets like vermin out of the woodwork.

Uncle Clyde unearthed a stash of booze from behind some sacks of grain and mixed an improvisational punch in the wheelbarrow. Albertha, who had been raised by drunks and married a drunk and mothered a drunk, allowed the circumscribed edges of her temperance to be tested and had a walloping big slug of Clyde's mead-thick, throat-scorching brew. The barn did a square dance around her, a dizzying reel, a three-hundred-and-sixty-degree *dos-à-dos,* before it settled back into place with everyone looking better for the ride, rosier of cheek and more companionable, arms reaching out for one another. All except for Billy Murphy and her boyfriend Douggie, who'd had a knockdown fight in one of the horse stalls and emerged with a matching his-and-hers set of shiners and split lips.

The master of ceremonies, Walter Kidd, rose on an overturned bucket to speak. "I've got dickall to say," he said. Earlier, in the orchard, he'd been sneaking peeks at his written speech when the wind ripped it out of his hands and posted it skyward. Walter himself was sailing higher than a kite. He told a meandering, off-colour yarn about a frog and a duck. "Which fits in here today, folks, with the, ahh… animal motive. Er, motif?" Next he proposed a toast, raising a dipper of hundred-proof in the general direction of the bride and groom, then promptly passed out, reeling off the bucket like a dead man. Everyone applauded heartily. Foot-stomping filled in for the tinkling of glasses, and a marital embrace boisterously demanded. As mother had wandered off somewhere, father turned to his best man and kissed him full on the mouth. "Oh, Morrie," his best man sighed, "Can't wait till later." Hoots and whistles filled the barn up to its beams and hung like high notes on the staff of wheat-coloured light that poured through the cracks in the wall.

The reception in full swing, it only took a bit of native ingenuity to transform the humble goods on hand into what was needed. Someone struck up a musical group, a tub-thumping, pot-banging, lid-smashing orchestra. The "concussion" section, as Clyde called it. Albert Richie found a rusty old saw and made it sing hauntingly, while Auntie Viv, never one to hide her light under a bushel, leapt onto centre stage playing her nose like a Hawaiian guitar. "You want Don Ho," she said, "you got 'im."

Spontaneous dancing broke out in several spots and Marg Petty threw herself into the burning heat of it, frugging and twisting and doing the limbo rock until her spine seized up and she couldn't move. Young Bobby wove among the guests with a basket of winter apples, and Billy Murphy worked the crosscurrent, holding one hand aloft and flat out like a platter. On it she had arranged bite-sized samples of her edible underwear. "Try one," she urged, while Douggie sat glowering on the sidelines, crunching handfuls of raw rice, his arm cast amorously around a sheep.

Albertha had gotten cornered by her cousin Barb, Tony's mother, who kept saying, "I don't understand it, I don't know *what* got into him. Tony's such a good boy."

"Uh-huh." Albertha was trying to listen to Barb with one ear and with the other catch those odd and enticingly incomplete snippets of conversation that were drifting her way.

"No guff, Ed, you got the greatest buns in town."

"Worried, you see, that I'd grow hair on my palms if I kept at it."

"He was never interested in girls. I used to say to him, Tony dear, you've got to get out and have some fun."

"And then d'you know what the crazy fool did? Ran out into the cornfield and buggered the scarecrow."

"What's long and hard and full of seamen?"

"Come again?"

"A submarine!"

"Ah," Albertha laughed. "Mind's in the gutter."

"Pardon me," said Barb, whose son happened to be elevated far above the gutter. He was up in the hayloft, in fact, with Mother.

Mother and Cousin Tony were entwined and adrift on a soft quilted chorus of drunken elation that rose from the party below. They had easily, and without much remorse, divested themselves of their clothing, scruples, and conventional notions of proper wedding conduct.

"Something borrowed," Tony whispered into Mother's knotted stook of yellow hair. "Something blue," he murmured, as he ran his tongue down her cheek, his burning hand over her breast, under her buttock. "Something old," he gasped, heart beating furiously, as they both did and conceived "something new."

Mother lay in Tony's arms, glowing, as though curled around an ember embedded in the sweet deep complexity of family life. She was thinking of beds made and unmade and made again. She was thinking about apple pies and mittens hung to dry by the stove and the howling wind in the chimney as she waited in the early winter dark for Father to come home, the old truck clunking up the road. She was thinking of fidelity, a bolt of pure white linen unwinding year after year after year. And she was thinking, *But oh, I like this better. Yes, I do.*

"You've got it backwards," she said.

"I do? Then turn around."

"No, silly, I mean the rhyme. It goes, something old, something new, something borrowed.... "

"Aw heck, I better get this thing right."

And Cousin Tony started all over again, this time taking a slithering nosedive down to nuzzle and kiss mother's delicate, unshod, and unclean feet.

Dissipated, weakened and aged, the wind muttered toothless imprecations around the barn, cussed softly in the eaves, and rattled the door ineffectually. It spun the weathervane listlessly and slid down the roof with a long, languid sigh. Night had begun to creep out of the furrows in the field, out of the shadowy clefts and recesses of the farm, with a slow hypnotic stealth. By the time it arrived in the orchard, drawing itself up to its full black height, the wind had vanished, having departed with a final skirling flourish through a curtain of air that now hung completely and serenely still.

Uncle Clyde threw open the door and Buckwheat appeared, a candy-coated apparition, wearing what was left of the wedding cake. As Clyde led him in, muttering under his breath, Lyle Sizer wandered over carrying a milk pail brimming with a rank, sludgy substance.

"Want some?" he said.

"What is it?" Clyde asked.

"I call it Cream of Bathroom Soup."

"Yeah? That's real nice. Why don't you go stick your head in it."

Continuing to mutter to himself, Clyde then tugged at an irritant long and stretchy that wound in and around his teeth. It turned out to be a chunk of elastic waistband from Billy Murphy's edible underwear. "Holy hell," he said, "more leftovers," deciding right there and then to pack it in.

"Goodbye," everyone was saying, "goodnight, goodnight," as they staggered through the door arm in arm, Young Bobby hugging a tailless, nameless, one-eyed barn cat. Albertha and Auntie Viv and Billy Murphy snuck out together, a snickering conspiring covey intent on skinny-dipping in the duck pond with a full evening of pranks to follow.

Father wandered out with them and then strolled into the orchard, hoping to find Mother, since she'd been missing for some time.

"Sweetheart," he called. "Honeybunch? Angel, where are you?"

The night and its more vocal residents, the crickets, cicadas, bullfrogs, and a baying hound, took up the unanswered plea and called, too, extemporizing and playing it for what it was worth, riddling the dark from every direction with a puzzled and troubled refrain. Where *was* she, they all wanted to know.

In response, and cutting through the insistent chirring and croaking and howling, came a sweetly melodic voice—although not Mother's—that said, most arrestingly, "Listen, listen, listen to *me*."

A mockingbird? A whippoorwill? A *nightingale*?

*No*, thought Father, *it can't be*. But gazing up into the old apple tree that arched above his head, he spotted him, a morning-coated, buff-bellied virtuoso come from miles and miles away to shivaree the bride and groom. "I'll be damned," he said." And he supposed he had the wind to thank for blowing the little foreigner so far off-course, for bringing them such a beautiful, golden-toned wedding gift.

Which is when he remembered Mother's name, the name that had eluded him all afternoon, that had slipped quickly away whenever he came near to grasping it. Now suddenly it was there in his head, spilling out of his mouth, branching upward into the night as he called out to Mother again, loudly and in high excitement, because he needed to share with her the small miracle of this presence in the orchard, this blessing, this omen of healing happiness to come.

# Momma Had a Baby

*And her head popped off.* My cousin Nile had spread himself out on the lawn, lethal as any chemical, and was decapitating dandelions with his thumbnail. Flicked sunheads spun haywire this way and that, ditsy blondes. *Momma had a baby* (pause) *and her head popped off* (flick). Another (flick) and another (flick). If the dandelions had been further along, he'd be blowing them bare, infesting everyone's lawns with his wishes, banks of yellow gold erupting days later, the flower of his desire for biceps, for cool cash, maybe a call from the Leaf's manager. ("Look, Keon's injured. We *need* you.") As far as nature was concerned, Nile was better than dogs' hindquarters, pant legs, and wind put together. Restless in fields, unwashed, he went about her pollinating business like a pimp. I felt for Nile the same degree of relatedness one might feel for a nightcrawler—a cousinage that had more to do with inhabiting the same stretch of earth than sharing anything as intimate as genetic material. But, ten years old, with an undescended testicle, Nile was the love interest, take it or leave it.

Inside was estrogen city, all women, mostly related, the air fibrous with connection. Even the few who weren't blood knew each other inside out, friends and neighbours who were practically sewn together, chain stitched with their knowledge and informed speculation about one another. Only one person stood on the edge of this dense familiarity like someone having an out-of-body experience—a woman who'd recently moved here from some smug Southern Ontario town and who appeared to have her jaw rusted shut. She was remembering, is all, lost to recollection. A younger sister who had succumbed to scarlet fever at the age of fifteen had arrived unbidden in her head and now after all these years rode there like a conquering whip-snapping queen in a chariot. Naturally, this gave her a somewhat self-absorbed expression.

The women were all packed into Auntie Viv's living room for a last minute, hold-your-breath baby shower. Very last minute, time stretched tight as a drum over Mother's huge belly. She was two weeks late and Auntie Viv thought this party might break the monotony, if not the water. Mother hoped not—her water that is— for she was beached on Viv's newly upholstered chester-field, formerly a spirit-lowering beige and brown tweed, now red and slick as an internal organ, enough colour and texture to make you giddy. Viv had put up bilious fleshy drapes to match, and Mother figured this show-off reason to be the real one for the shower, not her.

A fountain of dandelion heads spraying up outside, past the window, caught Mother's attention. *The Birth of Venus*, she thought, although she had only ever seen a commercial version of that famous painting, a picture in a magazine advertising shampoo. Still, wouldn't it be lovely, a freshwater baby rising out of the lake on a clamshell, dandelion heads flocking the feathery-soft air? So beautiful, so easy. Mother was terrified of dying in childbirth and understood her fear to be a restraining band, wide as a strop, holding her baby back. She entertained a morbid notion that already she had marked the baby, that it would be reticent and fearful all its life, and she prayed it would find a source of courage somewhere deep inside itself. If she lived, she resolved to call her baby Hero, boy or girl. If she died, Morrie would call it Stu if a boy, and Sue if a girl. That being the extent of it, Mother vowed to hold out *at least* until the naming formalities were concluded.

For her part, Auntie Viv was more than a little curious to see this baby, on account of Mother simultaneously losing her virginity and committing adultery scarcely hours into her marriage. She probably set some sort of record for the town, though it's not the kind of accomplishment you'd want to print up. Might be printed on the baby's face, mind you: Cousin Tony's visage appearing clear and crisp as a photograph, reproductive values more conclusive than the Shroud of Turin. This notion tickled Auntie Viv, for she considered her sister-in-law to be simpy and shallow as a pool. Piously nice. Let Mother pretend otherwise, but marriage had corrupted her, the cracks were beginning to show. Auntie Viv smiled her fox smile and wrenched her push-up bra back into place. Damn thing was chomping on her ribs *just like* something invented by a man.

When you think that Viv had cooked up this shower idea only the day before, Mother was getting a pretty good haul. Not that she needed more sleepers in neuter green or yellow—no one willing to commit her firm

opinions as to the baby's sex in material terms—or
teeny tiny vests (already outgrown) that made the whole
assembly chant *Awwww* when she held them up for
ritual gift inspection and approval. And, since this *was*
her fifth shower to date, she had enough fuzzy blankets and quilts at home to bury the kid alive. Most of
those present had contributed plenty to the prospective
infant, dearly hoping at this rate they weren't going to
have to fork out for its education, too.

My grandmother, Albertha Pinkham, veteran of the
four previous, knew enough to bring her gift in install-
ments. So far, the oddly shaped packages wrapped in
brown paper and stuck with adhesive contained wooden
slats, spindles, rockers, and a seat. She promised to knock
the rocking chair together and paint it once she had
the squalling evidence in her large sliver-flecked hands.
Albertha had ironed her linen dress for the first shower,
gesture enough she felt, and now it was so wrinkled it
might have been in pain. Gruesome. A sartorial senescence mimicking her own decline. She bowed her head
and dropped a brief prayer into the creases along the lines
of *No stupid games, all right? And do You think we could get
on with the show here?* By show, she did not mean more
teething rings and baby wipes, but contractions, a cre-
scendo of them, sudden and strong, a muscular fanfare
announcing the arrival of…. Glancing over at her child
stranded on Viv's hideous sofa, a giant's collapsed kidney,
she recognized that aura of fear, Mother's stricken look,
like that of an animal about to be clubbed. Albertha tacked
a stern postscript onto her prayer: *Remember, I go first.
Don't mess up.* How far afield had those rumours about
her daughter's infidelity drifted? Divine punishment?

Well really, grandbabies weren't so thick on the ground around here that anyone, divine or otherwise, should gripe if one came swaddled in a story or two. What was life without embroidery? Coarse cotton, that's all. Plain as unsullied paper, too plain for words.

*Momma had a baby . . .*

"What *is* that noise I keep hearing?"

"Nile, that lunk. Out on the grass."

*and her head popped off.*

Death, you know, crashing the party, mute as a shadow falling through the window. The uninvited guest. Which isn't exactly true, for my other grandmother, Gramma Young, had been issuing special invitations for years, beaming signals into the black depths of space, courting that one polygamous alien, violent lover, terminal seducer. Thus far she remained unrequited and a regular menace on the subject.

"My *last* shower," she sighed, sailing this hoary news across the room.

As this foreboding announcement was the very one she had made at the other four showers, no one was buying it. Any prior sympathies aroused had already been slashed to the bone.

"Mine too. We're *all* hoping that."

"Pine. A rough pine box, nothin' fancy for me."

"Chin up, Gramma. This is supposed to be a happy occasion. Think, real soon there'll be a new baby to cuddle."

"I'll never see it."

"C'mon, none of that talk now."

"New life comes into the world, old life's booted out."

"I'll drink to *that*," said Auntie Viv, agreeably enough, seeing as she'd been sneaking swigs from one of the flower vases she kept topped up with gin. The longevity of Viv's birthday roses always amazed Uncle Clyde, a phenomenon he could only attribute to some secret source of power generated by Viv herself.

"Tastes like soap," said Gramma Young, chewing with athletic effort one of Batty Pock's shortbread squares.

A message written in apologetic smiles, a kind of facial shorthand, flashed to Batty that said, *Never mind her, the old coot.*

Batty shifted uncomfortably in her chair. Whatever *had* happened to that soap powder, the cupful sitting on the counter when she'd been searching for the extra flour?

"*Mother*," warned Aunt Faith, seizing any opportunity to pay Gramma back, coin for coin, for every admonishing word she'd received as a child. Faith was the snappy sister, my least favourite aunt. She had resentment the way some people have religion—visibly—she wore it like a prow. If feeling slighted, overworked, neglected, she would take her husband Earl apart molecule by molecule, then reassemble him, a lesser man. She was Nile's mother, and he her son, and they fit together like a mathematical problem you could work on most of your life and never figure out.

*Drop dead*, Gramma was about to retort—she absolutely refused to let Faith have the last word—when, unaccountably, it *was* and she *did*. Drop dead. But a drop so slight, gentle as ash drifting down, it was as if a quieting finger had been placed lovingly on her heart to untrouble its agitated and relentless motion. Indeed,

Gramma had cried wolf for so long that her death was as tame and friendly as a panting, tail-thumping companion lolling at her feet. *I rest my case*, her body finally said, and in such an understated, such a gracious and accomplished manner, that no one, not even she, noticed her passing. She sat very, very still, and said nothing further.

Minnie Evans screamed, a startled little product, but only because Nile had smushed his face up against the window. Give him six years and he might almost resemble James Dean, but presently, features flatly pressed into the glass, he could have easily passed for a package of plastic-wrapped chicken thighs from the Red & White.

An intuitive awareness of something amiss perhaps sparked the inevitable birthing stories. Ancient Mariners all, women trotted out their individual traumas, sparing Mother nothing in their recollections of stillbirths, hemorrhages, Caesarean sections, and marathon labours. Babies' shrill kitten cries repeatedly stabbed the air, and gallons of lost, fictional, and phantom blood sloshed through the room.

My girl cousin, Amy, who had made a bow-hat out of an upturned tinfoil plate and the discarded gift bows, rose as if on a wave of this unsettling talk and placed it on Gramma Young's head. Her festive and improvisational bit of haberdashery slipped, caught on a stiff curl and came to rest at a rakish and merry angle.

"She's dead," said the woman from the south, who, until this moment, had not uttered a single word.

At least she spent her embarrassed verbal fund wisely. It was to the point.

"Pardon?" someone asked.

"What?"

"Good gravy! *Look* at Gramma Young."

"My arse," said Auntie Viv. "Stick a pin in her."

"Oh my God."

"She's only asleep."

"Faking it."

"No. No, I don't think so."

"Give her a nudge, Minnie."

"Not *me*."

"Heavens," said Albertha, reaching out to give Eve Young a wakening nudge, this *other* grandmother to whom she had rarely ever spoken, certainly nothing beyond courtesies. If you could call a grunt a courtesy. Truth was she didn't have time for whiners, and now she realized, touch telling no lie, that Eve didn't have time at all. It had withdrawn itself from her, its animating caress, its ticking breath.

They all shivered and stared at one another.

"I'll call Glanville, why don't I?" suggested Marion Goodwin, the undertaker's wife. Marion usually managed to appall and fascinate in about equal measure. What *was* it like being married to the Gland Man? This question swam up from a depth and circled visibly close to the surface. Imagine his unearthly cold hands reaching for you in bed at night (sheets reeking of formaldehyde), hands fat and grub-white that only hours before had been palpating the internal organs of corpses, drawing blood out of bodies with the same ease and indifference that they drained Freshie out of coolers at community picnics.

Marion wrote poetry, verse boxes that never seemed to contain humans, but heavily featured dewdrops, sunsets, and an array of symbols inert as stone markers. These she published in the town paper. *More embalmed mots*, the editor would groan when he saw her approaching down the walk, clutching yet another torso-thick bundle of paper in her arms, that unnerving pink smile of hers indelibly printed on her face.

"Viv," ordered Albertha, "call the ambulance."

"Hey," said Viv, as she sashayed out of the room. "Guess what? I've thought up a great name for a female comedy group." She stuck her head back in to deliver the punch line. "Titters."

An outbreak of giggles erupted and was quickly suppressed.

"Viv's in shock," someone said, kindly.

Someone else began to whimper, very quietly.

By this time Nile had taken off, pelting away like a hunted man. Soon he'd be tearing through fields, running and running, long grass singing past.

"It's coming," said Mother.

"So's Christmas," snapped Minnie Evans. A novice to the potency of sarcasm, she promptly fell apart, weeping buckets.

"What is, dear? The ambulance?"

"Already? Alec won't set out on a run till he's had a coffee and a smoke."

"The baby," Mother whispered. This a mumbled, prayer-faint revelation underlined by Alec's keening flashing progress down Viv's street.

"What baby?" demanded Aunt Faith.

Then a single dawning *Oh!* of recollection was all it took for everyone to fly into action. A dozen pair of hands rescued Mother from Viv's sofa, bundled her into

a shawl warm as a nest, and delivered her with mid-
wifely solicitations and endearments to the ambulance
revving its engine at the door.

One thing you have to say for it, the trip to the hospital was cost efficient. Not only did Mother, thrown
headlong into wracking convulsive labour, have to
share the ambulance with Gramma Young, cooling
rapidly and inviting no intimacies, but Alec stopped at
the Perdue's place halfway there to pick up pie-padded
Horace and wedge him in, too. Horace had swallowed
his pencil stub while working on a crossword. "*Women,*"
he confided to the male-grey upholstery into which his
face was pressed. You had to wonder if that was the
word he'd choked on filling in the puzzle, or whether he
considered his emergency eclipsed by the usual female
problems. Women, there was no escaping them.

And to prove it, I added my weight to the world.
Nine pounds, fifteen ounces of pure solid self. Mere
minutes after they wheeled Mother into the delivery room, some intern had me by the heels. Well. My
first bat's-eye-view of the situation was not consoling.
The room swung muzzy, as though rubbed in grease.
Mother lay bloody and limp, a brutalized body cast
aside. Pain seared my backside (never trust a doctor),
and I let go a river of sound, my tongue a flailing, undis-
ciplined instrument. But I must have known even then,
grabbing at the air—I had Albertha's hands!—that the
power would eventually be mine to carve that river into
the precise and commanding language I needed. For the
present, raw underspeech.

I said: *Mother, don't leave me.* I said: *Nile, get your
balls in order, boy. Your Hero's come to town.*

# Joie de Viv

When I was only a baby, carried around like a transistor on my father's shoulder, broadcasting the news—and there was plenty to tell, believe me—my Auntie Viv and I had an adventure. Tuesdays and Thursdays were my mother's "bridge" days. Everyone said it with the scare quotes attached like mini tattling tongues—or horns. Except Father, it not being in his best interests; to him bridge unadorned was the game she played, no questions asked, unalloyed truth a troublesome and unwanted article at the best of times.

On these days I would be dropped off at Auntie Viv's or Aunt Faith's. If the latter was my destination, apparent from the landmarks whipping past the car window, partly visible to me from my eyrie of blankets in the back seat, I'd start to fuss. This a mere prelude to a deafening, full-throated protest. For you see, I was a diva of the diaper set, a tot of a tragedian, and no one was more wronged than me. I could make the most amazing sounds, thereby unlacing the most tidily composed package of nerves, and I made them as the car sped along faster and faster, a grey shroud of dust

billowing up behind. If there's one message that children unheeded deliver repeatedly, it is: *unfair, unfair*.
They do this, speaking their outraged hearts for many
years, until finally they give up and start dishing it out
themselves. Anyway, *somebody* had to make Mother feel
guilty and I was never, but never, pleased to be dumped
at Aunt Faith's.

The moment Mother left, tearing out of the driveway in her hot haste, Faith would slap a strip of duct
tape across my mouth and say, "Don't think I'm gonna
listen to your yammering all day, kid."

If my cousin Nile was home and not out somewhere
in the world fine-tuning his delinquency, it wasn't so
bad. He'd carry me into the back bedroom, undress
me, and free of charge give me his complete attention.
I remain firm in my belief that his reasons for doing
so weighed more on the side of information than per-
version. I was his first naked girl and set the standard,
being anatomically perfect—a perfect babe, a postnatal
stunner, and I had great legs, if not yet ambulatory ones.
Besides, my family was not much for touching, which
is a failing in a family *and* in a pervert. The inspection
complete, he'd dress me again, all ass-backwards, and
we'd return to the kitchen, where he would station me
in his old highchair. First, he eased off the duct tape—
unlike Aunt Faith, who snatched it off like a Band-Aid
ripped off a wound as soon as Mother reappeared at the
door—and then, positioning himself at the other side of
the table, he'd begin to fire Corn Pops into my mouth.
Or tried to—most of them bounced off my forehead
or went wild. Once, he did manage to score with such
inadvertent precision that I gagged and choked. We

laughed uproariously at this, until I choked again. Well, that's the sort of stuff we did. It passed the time.

If on one of these bridge days we were clearly heading for Auntie Viv's place, I tried not to gurgle and babble overmuch on the way. The danger being that Mother might become jealous of my anticipatory happiness and turn back home, which had actually happened a few times. It's curious, but jealousy could accomplish what nothing else did—not maternal feeling, nor wifely duty, nor shame. If I hadn't been such an innocent, with the corresponding ration of lily-white brain cells, I might have used this insight to my advantage. I might have feigned the excessive delight for Faith's company that I only felt for Viv's, and spared myself much tedium and indignity. Conversely, as we headed to Viv's, Mother driving slower and slower and casting suspicious glances at me via the rear-view mirror, I should have performed one of my terror solos instead of waving my arms in excitement and beaming like an idiot. She could have used the reassurance of some heartfelt separation anxiety.

And Viv? Many years and a linguistic gap lay between us, but we spanned these distances effortlessly. Viv and I were mates and intimates, two gals together whooping it up. Talk? You've no idea. She stuck her duct tape where it belonged. I'd tell her my troubles, passionate in pre-speech, and she'd tell me hers. She filled me up like a bank with the coinage of her eventful and endlessly fascinating life. Fights with Uncle Clyde, grocery shopping, gossip with the neighbours, making-up with Uncle Clyde, psychiatric assessment of the neighbours ("That Mrs. Perdue is a friggin' nutcake"), not to mention detailed accounts of the health, well-being, and maintenance of her female equipment. If 'A is for Apple' and 'B is for Boy,' by the time you get to the X-rated end of the alphabet, let me tell you things get a whole lot more interesting. Not that I comprehended it all, but Viv's language had substance and shimmer and I caught the drift.

At home I was completely misunderstood. I could talk until I was blue in the face, and did, to no avail. My mother's friends circled around me, staring in fascination as though I were an accident (which, in fact, I was).

"Isn't she sweet," they said, interrogatively. "Does she ever stop talking?"

"No," said Mother. "Never."

If Father was within hearing range, he'd pipe up, "She's got brains, that one. Gonna be a lawyer. Real estate, law suits.… "

"Divorce," Mother said.

Father himself was a man of few words, but the ones he chose did the work of many, damming up whole flowing conversations, creating wary and fraught silences.

On the day of the adventure, I was miserable with teething and Mother was glad to be shot of me. She handed me over to Viv like a parcel to be posted ASAP. Her instructions were the usual ones, and were followed by the usual fiction concerning her whereabouts.

"Hey," said Viv, "we'll be fine. Enjoy yourself."

She meant it, too, being all for extracurricular activity. Why shouldn't a woman get what she needs elsewhere, when what she needs isn't a household item? Auntie did find it difficult to resist a dig, though, and added, "I suppose it gets *real* hard, eh? Bridge, I mean."

She snickered lightly like a bad fairy and held me closer. Then, with Mother a mere shadow in the door, good as gone, she whispered in my ear, "Hero, you and me doll, we're gonna have some kind of *fun.*"

And didn't I know it, for Viv's was a trust never broken.

Further on the subject of my teeth. Getting the buggers through would be worth it, I knew. Cut me a whole shiny set and the universe would be mine... but the procedure caused me much distress. If I could have articulated it, I would have used some of the foul language that Nile had been coaching me in for months, training me like a parrot. Given the pathetic reach of his aspirations, his one burning desire of the moment? That an obscenity would be the very first 'real' word I uttered. A blighted and bratty surprise for the parents. Thus far *uck, uck , uck* was the best I could do as a trash-talking infant, and I now strung these syllables out on a slick strand of spittle that bejewelled the fingers I had been so industriously gnawing upon.

One thing I admired about Auntie Viv: if you had a problem, she made a beeline for the most obvious solution. *Cut the crap* was a favourite expression of hers and pretty much summed up her approach to the unnecessarily complicated, be it a recipe for beef stroganoff, the emotional fallout from family strife, or theories of child-rearing. She instantly assessed my teething predicament, dipped her fingers into one of the flower vases where she kept a ready supply of gin, and rubbed this medicinal substance gently on my gums until I awarded her with one of my corporate, lawyer-to-be smiles. She dipped her fingers in again, crossed herself, then raised the vase and took a swig.

"Honey," she said, wiping her mouth on the back of her hand, "we're going for a ride!"

*A ride?* Great! We'd miss our soap operas, but no big deal, for the plot of Viv's life was equally engrossing and far less predictable. So when she said ride, I knew we weren't talking about a trip to the store to buy strained prunes.

In readiness we did the girl thing. Auntie Viv brushed my fawn wisps of hair up into a tiny scoop, teased it, and balanced it on top of my head like a dustball (more about dustballs to come). She attacked her own with a metal comb and a can of hair spray and in no time had crafted a do as beautiful as a Christmas ornament, golden and stiff, so hard that the wind glanced right off it when we hit the road, which we were shortly to do in Viv's old shit-coloured bomb. ("*Dijon*, sweetheart, we're two classy broads.") She dabbed my lips with crimson lipstick and smudged some on my chubby cheeks with her thumb.

"Cripes, what I wouldn't give for your skin, Hero. Faith got the good skin in our family, smoother than a baby's bum. No offence, eh. Course her face looks like a bum."

Next, alarmingly, Viv began to gouge at her eyes with a puny pair of tongs, which made her eyelashes stand up at a wonky and surprised angle, as though she'd faced a blast of considerable force. As she continued primping and painting—blue eyeshadow, mascara, the works—I had to wonder as I sometimes did if life wouldn't be better lived as a boy. But then, as Nile remained my only example to date of that particular state of being, there didn't seem to be much in the way of existential options. The human condition appeared to be as constricting a fit as a size small sleeper, a painful revelation.

Up to this point I had been philosophizing contentedly, but must confess that a complaint now escaped my unnaturally reddened lips.

"There, *there* honeybun, it's your old pal, Auntie Viv," she said, assuming that the bent eyelashes and makeup had made her unrecognizable to me. And, briefly, it was true, but not in the simple-minded way she thought. It wasn't *me* making strange, but life itself sticking its ancient, unknowable face menacingly in mine.

But like I said, Viv was direct, and directly she stuck a huge gobstopper in my mouth. "Here Mighty Mite, this'll fix you up." How right she was. She'd replaced unpalatable food for thought with an entirely sweet subject, one that caused me an immediate rush of elation.

Mighty Mite. That was a new one! I liked the names Auntie Viv gave me—some hilarious, some goofy, and all affectionately bestowed. They did somehow expand my play area and made more room for me to be. At home, Mother called me The Baby. As in, The Dog, The TV, The Toaster, and all the other sibling objects and creatures with which I co-existed. *Morland, The Baby needs a bottle. The Baby needs a change.…*

Yeah, right, a change of address.

"Almost ready." Viv grabbed her purse off the counter, a big old pussel-gutted sack of which I was extremely fond. A bag of wonders. When she flicked open the gold clasp and started rooting around inside, it exuded an intoxicating, powdery smell, like the

fragrance that sometimes gusted up, warm and soothing, from Viv's low-necked blouse. Lined with a black
silky material, watery-soft to the touch, its contents
were a bouillabaisse of ingredients that clattered and
clacked as Viv dug down deep and stirred everything
around. Among the items from this dragon hoard
that I'd been allowed on past occasions to handle and
mouth and shake were a compact, a bottle of Aspirins,
a nail file (*en garde!*—she swiped that one back), a box
of breath mints, a change purse, a hoop earring big
as a bracelet, a lighter, a rosary, a green rabbit's foot,
Tampax concealed in a mauve plastic case, a spare can
of hairspray, mirror sunglasses, a mickey of vodka, a
whistle, and a plastic troll with buggy eyes and hair
like a furry red flame... amazements all. This day,
after digging around for some time, making a cheer-
ful racket and muttering under her breath, Viv trium-
phantly yanked out her car keys and jangled them in
front of my face.

I laughed. Keys *are* funny, by the way. The ability to
perceive the humour in them is, sadly, something you
lose as you age... like your principles, and your marbles.

All a woman really wants to know about a car—
her identity not having bonded with a hunk of metal
on wheels—is where are the keys. Since we clearly
had those, and the tank full of gas, and the muffler more or less firmly attached (hockey tape), we
were set. Because the radio was broken, there'd be
no "Chug-a-Lug" or "Big Girls Don't Cry" or "Wild
Thing," but as neither of us were shy nor untalented,
we could belt it out without background assistance
from people in the biz.

*Grooovy, baby.*

Viv tossed a couple of beers and an extra bottle of formula into my diaper bag, slung her purse over her shoulder, and carried me out to the car. She settled me in front on a makeshift seat (bushel basket, pillows), hopped into the driver's side, gunned the engine, and we were away!

We streaked past the usual landmarks: the hydra-branched maple in the Perdue's yard that Nile would one day wrap his first car around; Parks' Variety, where a bounty of tooth-rotting delicacies awaited the arrival of my newly minted nippers; and the playground in which, abandoned in a buggy while Mother was off in the bushes, I often had to cool my heels and my temper while watching geriatric, three- and four-year-olds dashing around, acting mentally challenged, and having a ball.

As we headed into less familiar territory, I comprehended more fully the profound significance of this, my virginal voyage out into the wider world. Into the *unknown.* Thrilled and apprehensive, I could sense the bonds of home stretching as we zoomed along, and I speculated about how far one might go before they snapped altogether. Generally, members of my family were not travellers—their feet did not itch, except for medical reasons. The word 'wanderlust' made them blush, and to them the phrase 'the open road' only meant that the snowplow had been through and they could drive to town.

While I gaped at the sights like a slack-jawed rube—*A dog with spots!*—Auntie Viv yakked up a storm, part tour-guide, part teacher.

"Rock, Hero, over there, see the big rock. Can you say it, rock, rock? Tree. Tree, that's a tough one, eh? How about bird, bird… *bird.*"

How charming! No one else ever put any effort into pointing out such things to me, or encouraging the development of my oral skills. (Mind you, Father thought that I'd been born not only fully formed, but fully informed to boot.) The feeling was, I gather, that if I got hold of the language everyone else spoke there would be no peace at all, and that my discontent given voice would break us all asunder.

"Policeman, Hero! Po-lice-man. Doughnut. Dough-nut."

After the fuzz disappeared from view, Viv slowed down. She drew up to a guy standing on the side of the road who had one thumb hitched in the belt loop of his jeans, and the other stuck out, pointing in the direction we were headed. The clothing he wore must have been uncomfortably tight, his white T-shirt stretched like a sheath across his muscled chest, and he bulged elsewhere, too. When he spotted Viv behind the wheel, he smirked and gave her a cocky wave. In return, she gave him a squint-eyed and mirthless look. "And *that*, Hero, is an *asshole. Ass hole.* A genuine, one hundred percent *prick.*"

Ah, I thought, now this is more like it, more nuanced, and with a bit of math thrown in for extra educational value.

Viv had slowed almost to a stop and the guy swaggered over, mitt extended to the car handle. Then she hit the gas and we shot off down the road leaving Mr. Codpiece to duck a fusillade of tire-fired gravel. Viv seemed pleased about this gag and chuckled to herself, but didn't say anything until we arrived at a huge metal structure that spanned the channel. "Bridge, Hero. Bridge. We can play that game, too."

Our journey was a long one, and to fill the time we knocked back a bottle or two, counted out-of-province licence plates, woolgathered, and shot the shit. (Me, literally, which occasioned a roadside stop or two.) For some reason, Viv got to reminiscing about her old boy-friends—the lunch bucket, the meal ticket, the sweetie pie. You might think that the objects of her affection belonged in a cafeteria rather than in her heart, but in her heart they were firmly lodged, especially the sweetie pie.

"Mmm, what a hunk, one good-looking guy… and nice, Hero, *real* nice. He had this kooky name, Boniface, but we all called him Boner. Or Bony Part. He'd laugh. Great sense of humour. There's times, you know, I think to myself, Viv, *Viv,* why did you ever leave that boy? Why?"

Heck, everyone in town knew the answer to that. She'd had a fling with Uncle Clyde, got knocked up, married… and miscarried. Poor Viv, poor baby. She had me, at least, and I loved her like a mother, and my mother loved someone else, not like a child. Right this minute was my guess.

"So where is he now, I got to thinking? Lately, I've been kinda… I dunno, wondering." Viv pulled out and began passing a whole line of cars that were meekly trailing behind a logging truck poking along the twisty road. "What's he doing? I know he worked in the mines for awhile. Might have settled in the city. Did he get married, have kids?" She'd almost made it, when a car whipped around a curve on the other side, heading straight for us at top speed. "Did he ever get over losing me? It hurt him bad, what happened, ya know. Swore up and down he'd never forget me. Think of that." She jerked the wheel abruptly and forced the car into the slimmest of openings in the line of traffic, causing the guy behind us to brake and swerve dangerously, while leaning furiously on his horn. Viv, unruffled, casually gave him the finger. "So, you see, honey, I. . . ."

All very exciting, too exciting, for at this point, overcome with weariness, I fell into a troubled sleep, dream-stitching together the disparate images and impressions of the brimming day with uneasiness the only thread.

When I awoke, the car had stopped moving and Viv was no longer in it. Gone. GONE. Before I could work up a windshield-shattering scream, my attention was drawn by a *tap tapping* sound. Viv! Standing in a telephone booth directly outside and gabbing away to someone on the phone, she rapped on the glass, while at the same time waggling her eyebrows at me. I replied by waving my arms joyfully and kicking my feet like crazy, until one of my fucking booties flew off.

"Uck!" I said. "Bork!"

"Hey, kiddo! We're on." Viv slid back into the car, twitchy with excitement. "Easy peasy, who woulda thought." She peeled away from the curb without looking behind to check for traffic, causing more brake-squealing and horn-blatting, to which she seemed completely oblivious.

More houses than I had ever seen before flashed past—houses and stores and more houses and throngs of people and traffic and fast food joints and lights and signs. The enormity of it all left me speechless. While no more than a grungy, down-on-its-luck mining town, it was no less an eye-opener (and lip-zipper) to me than a tour of New York would have been. Auntie Viv had gone quiet, too, and her colour was high. She drove on at a clip and smoothly navigated a maze of streets as if pulled along by some otherworldly force. And truly, I had the discomfiting sensation that the reality of the day had sprung a few leaks.

Viv pulled into the driveway of a poky, stuccoed, heart-sinker of a bungalow and parked behind a battered, hearse-black station wagon. The house, as I say, had a dispiriting air, in that it was too determinedly neat and tidy. A battle against entropy had been waged here with limited resources. Fortunately, I didn't have to look at the place as Viv strode toward it. She held me snug against her chest and I could feel her heartbeat quickening. With her past slam-dunking into her present, it was one active organ in there trying to keep time with her expectations.

A white plastic deck chair sat on the front stoop awaiting an arse to fill it. As Auntie Viv always needed lots of room to manoeuver, she nudged the chair off the stoop with her knee and it toppled over onto the buzz-cut lawn, legs in the air—an easy victory. The very second she rapped on the door, it jerked open and we were greeted (hardly the right word) by a woman of some heft and no evident charm. She blocked the threshold, adopted an arms-folded, combat stance, and aimed her small eyes at us as though her face were some sort of weapon. Craning my neck around to stare at her, I knew for certain that if there were any children at all in this household they were simmering in pots on the back stove.

"Yah?" she said. "You the one who called?"

"That's me," said Viv brightly. She tried peering around the woman to see inside, as did I. I could hear pot lids rattling in the kitchen, the kids escaping as steam. "Boniface in? You said he was home."

The woman glared at her. And then—at *me*.

"Boner?" Viv tried again. "I'm an old friend of his, like I said."

"Boner, is it? Nah, he's not *in*. He's *in* somewheres else. Ya know, you gotta nerve callin' up like that. I wanted to see what one of his gals looked like. And I'll tell you somethin', you're not so hot. You're an old friend all right, *real* old."

Viv now gave this woman a closer and more discerning inspection, as though examining fecal matter for undigested roughage. "Pardon me," she said.

"You heard me." Then indicating me with her chin, "Don't try to tell me that's his brat, neither. I know what you're after and you're not gonna get away with it. Good Lord , look at it, *look at it*. It's got rouge on. Nuthin' but a little *whore*… just like its mother."

This may have been true about my mother, but having been reduced to an "it" and an it-of-the-night at that, I personally wasn't feeling overly well-nourished by the milk of human kindness, and dearly hoping—and expecting—that Auntie Viv would punch this witch flat as a carpet. Instead, Viv shoved the woman aside and breezed into the living room. She headed straight to a monster sideboard that had an oppressive bank of family photos arrayed on top.

"Hey," the woman shouted. "Where d'you think you're goin'? You can't come in here."

Viv plucked a heavy, gaudily framed photograph out of the very heart of this morbid assembly, all mop-topped, shiny-faced hag spawn. She studied the picture with an utterly neutral expression. You had to admire her control, for the object in hand was a wedding photo, *the* wedding photo.

"Got an eyeful? Satisfied? He loves me, see. Always will. Not that it's any of yer business." The woman gave her housedress a fastidious tug. "So go stick your big nose somewhere else."

The *cow*. This news must have pained Auntie Viv something awful, but gazing up at her I saw the tiniest flicker of amusement cross her face. She stepped back quickly and in so doing snagged a dustball from underneath the sideboard on the pointy toe of her shoe. Slut's wool, as Aunt Faith calls the stuff, a domestic and poor-woman's version of the golden fleece, although this one was distinctly penile in shape and remarkably long. More hare than bunny. We both gaped at it.

"Holy," Viv snorted. "A big one."

Our hostess, patchily red in the face and moist of upper lip, responded to this compliment in an oddly compressed tone, as though she were cooking her tongue in her mouth. "*Get out,*" she said. "*Get out of my house or I'm callin' the police.*"

"You do that, honey," said Viv, and holding out the picture frame in her hand like a plow, she cleared the sideboard of family members, wiped it clean. Away they went—briefly taking flight before smashing onto the floor, picture glass cracking and shards spraying up. "That's better." And for good measure, she next cleared the coffee table of knickknacks: a souvenir ashtray from Niagara Falls (where else?), a fussy maroon candy dish covered in a rash of glass bumps, two Blue Mountain pottery swans, a ceramic bulldog with mad, mismatched eyes (which I kind of liked), and a duo of cheapo figurines. "Can't stand this tacky garbage, can you Hero?"

It did look much better in motion, a flurry of fragments, beaks, arms, and tiny heads on the roll. Action kitsch.

By this time, the lady of the house had found her voice again and was screaming her own head off, auditioning for a heart attack. Viv tossed the wedding photo onto the wreckage and we were out of there. She skedaddled to the car as fast as one can in high heels, but before hopping in, stopped behind the station wagon and kicked out its back lights. *Ha!*

In a jiff, we were roaring down city streets, squealing around corners, laying rubber like outlaw girl stars in a car chase scene. Only no one was chasing us. Viv appeared flushed and animated, so alive there seemed to be sparks flying out of her golden helmet of hair. After a bit, she slowed down, saying, "No cops? Huh, maybe the old douchebag passed out, cut her head on the glass and bled to death."

I chortled.

Then she shrugged and said, "Heh. Wrong guy."

"Waaaa?!"

"How was I supposed to know? Name's in the phone book. Boner's name, his first *and* last, how common is that? Smith, sure, there's a bunch of those around, but his first name, eh. Boniface, eh. That's real different." Viv cracked a smile. "Man, her hubby's gonna catch it when he gets home. The *cheat*. Can't say as I blame him… hey wait, did you hear that? Listen."

Auntie Viv slowed almost to a stop while we attended to a thin whine, a needle of a sound that quickly grew louder, more piercing, closer.

"Uh-oh," she said, picking up speed again. She skimmed along for a stretch, looking left and right, assessing side streets for potential hideouts. Sundry exhilarating zigzags later, she took a sharp turn, restraining me with her arm so that I wouldn't fly like a putto out of my apple basket, and passed through a pillared gate with a wrought-iron sign arching overtop that read (for those who can do it): Laurel Grove Cemetery (with not a laurel in sight). We drove some distance down a lane until we came to a squat stone house that looked like a Palladian home for midgets. Viv pulled in beside it, which concealed the car from view. While the old bomb sputtered and eased into silence, she sniffed once, twice, and then turned to me, saying, "Something stinks."

Too right. I'd been engaged in my own dirty business back at the scene of the crime, and was gratified to be finally receiving some credit for it. Efficient in this as in all else, Viv soon had me stretched out on a bench, making small talk while she worked (saving me face *and* rear), pausing to listen as the siren passed by the cemetery and then diminished in the distance. This made her chuckle again—I loved the low rumble of it—and she gave me a quick wink. Job done, she hoisted me up into her arms and we started to stroll along the grassy pathways, surveying the headstones in a mildly curious way, occasionally stopping to read an inscription. Her mood was light, her interest in these terse biographies detached and scant. We sauntered past low hillocks and humps, wandering through this decorous and orderly gathering of final selves as if it were a normal and pleasant place to take a constitutional.

But there was danger here, and it found us.

One minute Viv stood at a safe enough distance, completely untouched, and the next that distance had slammed up against her, a fist to the chest. I felt her flinch, then stagger slightly. She whirled around—I saw no one, no deliverer of shocks, no stinging wasp—and she retraced her steps hurriedly, almost at a run. Her heart again, and again, her feet, faster, faster.

"God," she said. "*My God.*" We arrived back at the bench and she sank down, gingerly, as though she had grown suddenly frail. It was so unlike her that I let go a whimper, and she gripped me tighter. "Don't mind me, Hero. It's nothing. Nothing," she repeated. But this nothing was not empty—it had cold contents. I shivered. She held me so close that her pores aligned with mine and I began to feel her alarm filter into me, filling me up like an urn. I had hardly enough body to contain it, this adult overflow of grief. "I never knew," she said. "All these years… and *no one* told me?" I began to wail, and so did she. We wept noisily like this for some time, until we were interrupted.

Rudely interrupted, in my view, although Viv seemed to welcome it.

A man in a dark suit stood over us, an expression of sympathy and concern on his face. A striking face, a dissembling face. How did I know this? Well, I wasn't born *yesterday*, was I?

"I'm so sorry," he said. "Is it a loved one? Can I help?"

Auntie Viv shook her head and wiped her eyes, smearing the sleeve of her blouse with streaks of Maybelline. "Thanks, no, I'm okay," she said, followed by a loud sniff.

He smiled. Her age I'd say, and yes, very handsome, debonair streaks of white in his dark hair. Tentatively, she smiled back, and then set me down beside her. *Mistake!*

"Boy or girl?" he asked pleasantly, nodding at me, the indeterminate it.

"Girl. Isn't she gorgeous?" Nice complement, but Viv's tone was off, kind of flirty. She *liked* this guy?

"She's very pretty," he said. "Like her mother."

Oh, come *on!*

Viv tittered.

*No, no, no!*

He reached out to scrumble the fuzz on the top of my head and I shrieked. *Get squashed, troglodyte!*

"Ignore her," Viv said, treacherously. "She doesn't know you is all."

The man opened his hands, Jesus-style, and made his pitch. "We could remedy that. I'd love to buy you two ladies a refreshment. There's a café not far from here, a great spot. They serve spirits, too, if that's your fancy. What do you say?"

*Say no. Please.*

"Hmm, gee, I dunno. We should be getting back. I suppose one drink wouldn't hurt.… I could use a stiff one, if you wanna know the truth."

Ha, ha. *Christ*, Viv.

The man clapped his hands together, producing a final, bargain-with-the-devil *crack* that made me wince. "Wonderful. Might as well take my car."

"Sure, yeah. I'll grab my purse."

As Viv hustled over to our car, the man bent down and stared at me, his gaze entirely altered. I was petrified.

"Stupid little bitch," he said quietly.

Viv returned pronto, digging deep in her purse. Her medicine pouch, her bag of tricks. "Want a smoke?"

The man stood up, quickly resuming a kindly expression. "Thanks, but no, not for me. Gave it up years ago."

"How about *this* then?"

Viv whipped out her spare can of hairspray, got her trigger finger on the nozzle, and gave him a full blast in the face. She sprayed him like a bug and he crumpled like one, groaning, hands over his eyes, too shocked and pained for immediate outrage. Quickly, *quickly,* she snatched me up from the bench and took off, her nails digging into me. Once again we were on the run, in the car, roaring through those black, woeful gates, and *gone*.

"Vivivivivivivi." You hear what I'm saying? My name may have been Hero, but she, Viv, was mine once again.

And to seal it, she said, "Aw, hell, sweetheart. Let's forget that slimeball and go for some ice cream."

On the outskirts of the city, she pulled in at a fast food stand. After she got out of the car and retrieved me from the other side, we waited in line behind a party of nuns who were all dressed in white and speaking French. They were incredibly lovely, I thought. Unhurried and serene. I was entranced by their exotic language and by how the wind moved among them, fluttering their white habits and veils. Every single one of them ordered vanilla ice cream cones and we did, too, to be companionable, although I'm more of a Bubblegum person myself, and Viv's a Tiger Tail. We stood around smiling and nodding at the nuns, and they smiled and nodded back, and we all sucked contentedly on those sweet, pure, melting scoops of ice cream. I tell you, it did our hearts and souls a wondrous amount of good.

The only downer? We were late in getting home. But then, Mother was late, too.

Very. "My late mother," I might have said if I could have, only it wasn't death that took her.

# Bigmouth

## 1

There was a time in my extreme youth when I stopped speaking. I'd had my say. Enough, enough. One day I paused in mid-sentence to take a breath and a great tide of air rushed into my mouth and bore my words back up into my brain. Keep them, I thought. Burnish them to a higher sheen and hoard them. Mark this (I also thought): the time will come when my detractors will crawl to me on hands and knees, their heads empty as beggars' bowls, pleading for *one wordy crumb, that's all!*, some paltry token from my vast—and by then compounded—investment.

But, my spendthrift days were over. For years my silver tongue had tolled almost unstoppably. I could be absolutely relied upon to deliver commentary on failings of family life, along with critiques and crisp assessments of anyone who lived within shooting range. Besides this, I tossed off clever asides on more general themes, likewise aphorisms, puns, and *bon mots* that were sheathed in the luminous and crackling golden foil of my wit. Mine was a richness of expression known around the house, otherwise and regrettably, as Hero's "prattle" or "gibberish." To say that I was underappreciated does not even begin to say enough. My mother had taken to stuffing cotton balls in her ears and wearing earmuffs, or breaking out into spontaneous acts of vacuuming whenever I cleared my throat. Father was more receptive and attentive, although after listening to me for an extended period, his face would take on a worn and exhausted expression, as if what I had to say made no more sense than what the wind had been saying forever to the eroded brow of the shore.

So, I paused. I paused and silence fell among us. Like a benediction, I gather. At first my parents looked around inquisitively, blinking like Sleeping Beauties newly awakened, faint, puzzled smiles forming on their lips, for they couldn't quite identify what was happening. Then simultaneously—and guardedly—they looked at me. I went about my business, pulling the head off my doll and snapping it back on with a gratifying *pop*. (Perhaps I'll become a doctor instead of a lawyer, I mused, considering how my communicative skills will no longer be exercised.) I knew what they were thinking. Not that I might be unwell, or sick at heart, or conducting a protest, or suffering an artistic crisis—speaker's block—but, that carried along by some unheralded developmental surge, I had passed through my yakkety-yak phase, my prolonged and painful bout of verbal colic. They were thinking—now that they could hear themselves do it—that I had finally become a bonafide member not only of our family, but of the whole human community. I had become normal, that is. Which is to say, repressed and fumbling and ever proving the lamentable inadequacy of language as it is usually deployed.

So much for providing a domestic service. Fine, I clamped my lips together: let them speak to one another and see how far they get. I refused to supply the linguistic binding that might have held this whole fragile structure together. Rents, rifts, leaks. A family needn't be airtight to float, sealed up so snug you can't breathe, black emotional pitch in the seams, but there were drafts in ours, cold currents circulating that had an alien source. I knew what was what, if not precisely the meaning of what I had witnessed: my mother reaching through a bombed-out hole in the wall of our family into the raw, hard light of day, and placing her hand gently as a fallen leaf on the back of a stranger.

I wasn't the only talker among my relations. During family get-togethers my Uncle Clyde spoke in tongues, providing he had enough fuel in him for liftoff. Cow's tongue, chicken, pig—he could do a fair imitation of my grandmother Albertha's sow, Maud. (Massive Maud, a fleshy and sensitive pink nestled in straw, all tongue she could have been, a huge speaking organ.) Clyde grunted and oinked and squealed—throat slit, Easter dinner—making a comedy of these sad, irreligious sounds. He did this mainly for the benefit of his sister-in-law, my Aunt Faith, a real tongue-banger herself, who'd been reborn (whereas *I* got it right the first time around) and on the subject of religion was merciless.

"Tell me, I'm inerested here, what's the difference between praying and braying?" Clyde queried before performing the latter and rolling his eyes heavenward.

"Give it a rest, Clyde," Auntie Viv said, with a snort of laughter, while Faith cursed him and predicted that one day he would be struck dumb.

Instead, it happened to me, or so they must have reasoned. Me, who had so often broken the rules designed to silence children: don't speak with your mouth full, speak only when spoken to, a child should be seen, not heard. Then if you did clam up, they shamed you for not speaking.

"What's wrong with *you*?" Faith said. "Cat got yer tongue?"

*Nope,* my answer under normal circumstances, *bird got your brain?* But I would not be drawn. Any confidences I had to divulge, I shared with the local fauna. This included our pumpkin-coloured dog, E.D. Smith (he *was* the exact shade of the pie filling, but named after our mayor Ed Smith, who'd been caught pissing against the side of the town hall), and my cousin Nile, who was wayward enough to be counted in with the wildlife. E.D. Smith was highly receptive, a diplomat of dogs, human affairs to him as diverting as a steaming pile of dung. Lifting the velvety trapdoor of his ear and whispering to him, I could hear my secrets drifting slowly down into the cellar of his canine soul. Nile was another matter. He didn't care. I tried to tell him what I heard late at night, the sounds that skirled up into my room. My parents arguing, a violent jagged drone, a crude hornet's nest of words kicked against the wall.

"Turn around Scuts, let's play our game."

He lifted my shirt and began to draw pictures on my bare back with his finger. It only felt like tickling to me, but the object of the game was to guess what he was drawing. Or who he was drawing, as his quick sketches had lately evolved from cars into curvy female shapes. 'Nuds,' as Uncle Clyde would say, the stripped nymphs of Nile's distorted local mythology.

"Roxanne Box?" I guessed.

"Nah, not enough room on a skinny minnie like you for that tub of lard."

"Peg Ritchie, then."

"Her? She's a dog. C'mon Scuts, it's easy."

"Draw her again."

He ran his finger, nail ragged and scratchy at a real nib over my shoulder blades, down my spine, trunk to waist, his medium as he drew the lineaments and filled in the details of this softly rounded mystery woman. She evaporated the instant he laid her down, and yet, and yet... didn't I know her? She felt familiar, close, so lightly riding on my back. A burden of absence, not weight. Who was she?

"I give up," I said, hating to, hating to let Nile win.

"Waa, waa," all he'd say. "Sucky Baby's gonna cry."

There were questions I could have asked if I were on speaking terms with the household and the world at large. A child could whine like a dog (or a mayor) at the closed bedroom door.

The sounds they made in there were scarcely to be believed. Animal grammar, I could write the book.

My mother had many admirers. Or maybe it was only one, unrecognizable, mercurial, his face always turned away from me, or bagged in shadow. That half-man who slipped out the back door like a thief. Once I saw his hands gripping the sides of her head like a vice. I saw her own hand pressed hard against his face, the heel of it in his mouth.

I'd been told, often, not to speak to strangers. Uh-huh. In my own home? I wondered if this prohibition was some sort of sly joke, or intended as good advice that my own mother had not heeded, to her peril. Before taking my vow of silence, speaking had come as natural to me as breathing. No one had warned me before of its dangers, how it might draw predators to the door.

"She's changed," I overheard my mother telling Auntie Viv. "For the better. She's much quieter, shy all of a sudden. Growing up, I guess. For a while there, I thought she'd never shut up."

"I dunno, I don't like it," said Auntie Viv. "It's like she's in shock, eh, like she's *seen* something. Something bad. *Real* bad."

E.D. Smith moaned softly in his sleep, his legs twitching, enduring dreams of doggy council meetings, endless and inescapable. A cloud of flying ants drifted by the window, the mating aerial relations of the ones that were undermining the front porch, turning solid woodwork into lace. I could hear them if I placed my ear against the floorboards, a light scratching within, disaster arriving in increments.

Mother laughing. A beautiful sound, but only she was making it.

Okay, so what if I talked? Carefully, casting a spell over the house without wasting myself, only enough language to effect the necessary repair.

Too late, though. Too late to hold it fast and tight.

Now see, I told you this would happen. A time came when my father fell on his knees, suitor-style, before me. He grabbed my arms, my inoffensive and listening father, and shook me hard, desperate for the treasure I contained.

"Where is she? Hero, you know, tell me. *Where?*"

So we've descended to this, I thought. All right, I'll tell. And for once in my life I was succinct. I sifted through those months of silence for what they had to offer, and said, simply, "Gone." No gem, no gold, but a ghost of a word, a word without habitation. Wind whistling down an open plain, a tire track in the sand, a wisp of exhaust trailing off into nothing.

## 2

Once a man came walking along our shore. I had put in a full morning ransacking my parents' room, clawing through drawers, looting the jewellery box, yanking dresses off their hangers in the closet, tossing out shoes. It was an approach, what was I supposed to do? You can't make a mother out of lipstick, spilled perfume, and a sweater set laid out flat on the floor, but you can doll up her absence. I wrote a ransom note using the nub of an eyebrow pencil. I painted the puppies' toenails red and powdered their faces until they started to sneeze. Sometimes Father was too smart for our own good. But mostly he was too stupid. He named them Romulus and Remus. Somebody had dumped them at the end of our road, two pups in a sealed-up cardboard box, passing their problem along with a callousness that was pervasive enough in the world, but usually missed us gormless rubes, suckers who couldn't resist opening a whimpering, barking box.

Not yet up to a macho, snarly toothed show of aggression, the pups were too young to save my life, but they at least provided a brief, clownish diversion. Not long after Mother disappeared, E.D. Smith, our old, orange mutt, went missing, too. Lost in the bush, Father said. This unregulated passage of people and animals made the unknown man's arrival less unexpected to me than perhaps it should have been. By then I was outside, near the dock.

"Hello girl," he said.

Girl? No one had ever called me *that* before. He was unshaven. His eyes were bloodshot, his clothes what you might expect—filthy white T with a ripped flannel shirt overtop, work pants, a nap of motor oil and dirt where he'd wiped his hands on his thighs, scuffed boots, half-unlaced. In short, your classic stranger (hick model), literally the kind of child-stealer and abominator that mothers conjure up to terrify themselves with. But the thing was, you see, I didn't have a mother. Sure, there were intimations of her. She lingered still in the house, in the folds of the curtains, in the depths of the burnt-bottomed pots and pans. *My Sin*, unstoppered, gave you a good strong blast of her. Her soiled slippers, her hair snaking through a brush, her pink swimsuit in the bathroom slung like a piece of skin on a nail. But not *her*. She was the crime for which she had left too much evidence.

The puppies did their best, tumbling white-faced around the corner of the house, a mother parody with their red nails, cheap clip-on earrings swinging low on the tips of their floppy ears, the sweater set divvied up between them. The man stared at them, unmoved by their canine youth, undeceived by their disguise. He then stared at me—much too long. Calculating, I suppose. Doing the books, assessing my value, my silence, my availability. He was unsmiling, shrewdly serious, not wasting any charm on me. He had come by the shore, not the road, but he hadn't made a game of it, hopping from rock to rock as I would have done. So what did he conclude finally?

*No, not this one. This one's trouble.*

For all I knew, he could have been an acquaintance of my father's, looking for him. Or some harmless sap looking for a job, a drifter, a lost soul. Although really, how many times do you have to learn not to be taken in, and yet you go ahead and open that can of worms, that taped-up box?

He wasn't fooled, at any rate. I *was* trouble. Trouble's apprentice, and trouble's little cousin. I was being coached in it and had become a true disciple of the condition. A loquacious smartypants when younger, Father had told everyone that I was destined to become a lawyer. Since then I had learned to dummy up, but law still interested me, especially the other side of it where my cousin Nile ranged, secure in his delinquency, beckoning.

This girl business, though, I didn't like it. Other people were accusing me of it, too, if more indirectly. Insinuations were being made.

"Did that man speak to you?" barked Aunt Faith, after I skipped back into the house.

Barked was her usual mode of expression. That, or snapped, growled, scolded, sneered. She never just said. Behind the tight set of her jaw, she had a cache of unpleasant information stored, a jackpot of sordid particulars that she did not intend to share with me. Mind you, it must have been tempting. She would have enjoyed scaring the wits out of me.

"No."

"You be careful, hear."

"Why?"

"Never mind."

"But why?"

"Don't ask."

Speak and die, was that it? Speak to a stranger and he'll hold your innocent response taut as a cord against your throat.

I wasn't all that surprised to find Aunt Faith in our living room, spying on me. Since Mother left it was like open house at our place. Female relatives streamed through with casseroles, ironing, advice, lies. I never realized before that one woman in the house protects you from others.

"That girl of yours, Morland, heard tell she was out by the lighthouse. . . ."

Breaking windows? Check. That part was true. I broke the sun in them, shattered them into blackness. I was handy with a rock. But that other thing, they weren't going to pin that on me. It's not that I wanted to be a boy, what good would that do? I wanted to be something larger, looser, something that would take in the puppies, and the shore that man walked along, and the hidden, twisted road that took my mother away from me. Call me *that* and maybe I'd listen.

Nile, lean and quick, slipped unseen through the dark, a wolf in wolf's clothing. At night, lighting matches on his teeth, he might have been pulling fire right out of his mouth. A couple of barns went up that summer. We watched them go, faces doused in orange light.

Romulus ate Father's Y-fronts and Remus caught hell. There was a useful lesson in this, I felt, but not having a sibling of my own, I didn't know how to apply it. I had to bear the guilt of Mother's defection, there being no other child around to blame but me. Children squabble over their parents' attention, and when there is no attention at all, you get to eat dust, however many there are of you. No attention stretches pretty far. Father didn't mean to withdraw, but he was stricken. There was a dearth in the family. (Some joke.) Like me, he was missing some pertinent, possibly saving, piece of information. He didn't know what to do, so he kicked the dog, which is what they're for, according to Aunt Faith. Then later, because he's a soft man pulled out of shape, he apologized. He took Romulus' paw in his hand and murmured affectionately to him. But again, wrong dog. Crime rewarded. Tail thumping, Romulus grinned quizzically, the single beneficiary in our house of civilized behaviour. Shreds of Father's Stanfield's were snagged like floss in his teeth.

And on the subject of unmentionables, you didn't want to turn your back on Nile, a great one for stealing up behind you, silent as smoke, sliding his hand down the back of your jeans, and giving your gotchies an abrupt, often vicious, yank. A corny and puerile trick that drove the crotch up into your crack like a G-string. It hurt. It was humiliating. You had to laugh, though.

"How could she *walk* in these?" Caught snooping in my parents' room, Aunt Faith snatched up one of Mother's spike-heeled pumps and shook it at me.

She could. She did.

"Dog's breakfast, this room. It's disgusting."

Woof, woof.

This occurred to me—her leaving was the ultimate maternal act. Altruistic, a sacrifice. She did it *for me.* Her defection protected me from harm, far more that her anxious presence would have done. Breaking rules (and windows), telling fibs, watching, waiting, I had grown wary and more observant. Watching the road, the shore. There are worse things than being raised by wolves.

When Remus was older, he developed this habit of jumping on car hoods. We all ran wild, but he took it further, as though wildness itself were a country whose boundaries he had to leap clear of. A mad lilt feathered his heels, a death wish gleamed in his eye. Men don't like to lose their women, don't like them touched or tampered with. The same applies, only double, to their cars. Dirt on the whitewalls makes them unhappy. A missing hubcap is a quest that can take days of ditch exploration. Rust eating a fender, scratches on the hood, don't even think about it. As Remus skidded across the hood of Nile's waxed and polished black Buick, he left behind a fatal trail in the paint, an empty musical staff, scoring for a dirge. Like a cartoon dog, he skated *scritching* across the hood until he stood eyeball to eyeball with the driver, pallid face looming on the other side of the windshield. Remus, the unlucky one, the dupe. He did not disappear in a thunderstorm and enjoy deification, as did his brother's namesake, but disappear he did, not long after.

Father read the ransom note I wrote in eyebrow pencil *Leave money under doormat.* (WELCOME the mat said in big rubber letters, although we didn't really mean it. GO AWAY was more the idea.) I didn't specify the amount, not wanting to undervalue myself by asking for too little. I did add, *Or Else!,* implying perhaps that if he didn't pay up he'd find me at the end of the road, my remains sealed up in the now vacant cardboard box. Or found not at all, my whereabouts never to be revealed.

Father smiled and dug into his pocket for some loose change, which he slipped under the mat. "For candy," he said aloud, thinking, *My poor motherless daughter.*

*For ciggies,* I smiled, watching him through the window, thinking, *Poor dumb Dad.*

*I'll leave him too, first chance.*

And you know what, I *did* speak to that man, that loathsome stranger. I even acknowledged the identifier: *girl.*

"Hello," I said. "Mister."

It wasn't much, but he knew what I meant. *Hello* danger, depravity, bearer away of female bodies, whoever you are. You've found me, so young, but yes, it's *me,* and I'm ready to go, too. *Hello,* welcome, here are my hands, take them, and my child arms. Let me embrace you.

# Dream House

Forget me, down the hall in the back bedroom, locked in a deaf and dumb innocence, a useless daughter. The light from the approaching car struck the window and then swept over me, a bright, quickly vanishing cloth. A branched silhouette from the tree outside sprang into shadow-life and skimmed along the walls. Missed it. I was sunk in a pit, some deep night-hole into which I'd fallen without resistance, that being the idea, after all. Sleep, sleep, sleep. Let her fend for herself.

The sky was clear, star-engorged, and she'd been standing at the picture window in the living room for some time, staring into its clarity. I didn't know this. I didn't know anything, and despite my famous volubility, wasn't even mumbling prognostications in my sleep. Father said I was as bad as a fishwife, tongue like a file. He pretended pain, ear-sores, abscesses, as I rattled—and ratted—on. An incessant, rasping tale-bearer—such was my reputation, if not my true profession. Call me, rather, the CEO of secrets, the administration of which comes at a cost. His real wife, the prodigal wonder, was slippery as a fish, although no creature compound. She stood on one side of the glass, her wide mouth working, letting soundless cartoon bubbles of distress escape.

She had her reasons. She was lousy with cause. A woman alone in the country, unprotected, with a child asleep in an upstairs bedroom. A child she may have even loved, who knows. Don't look at me. Not my affair. I was more an adjunct to her story, like a distant, irritating fixture on the house, a loose drainpipe that rattled in the wind.

She stood by the window, watching, one hand at her side, thumb ranging nervously over her cuticles, her nails, extremities to which in calmer times she paid more focused attention, painting, buffing. Lunulae never obscured by the incremental drift of dead skin. A slender hand, pretty, unlike her mother's more manly, squarish one, and unlike mine, spidery and busy, fingers twitching as I slept. A fair amount of damage had been caused nonetheless by her more delicate hand. If her marriage was a cage, she knew her way around its latch.

A woman's story, then. Inconsequential, no one wanted to hear it. Although it had made the rounds of town, gaining in girth, accruing some fantastical features. Her history had become a garish, hopped-up lure that might easily have drawn a carload of drunk, out-of-control males down our road, bouncing in the ruts and potholes, fishtailing on the loose gravel.

But this car that turned off the main road and headed down ours was more measured in its approach, its driver cooler than cool. If that can be determined from a motoring style. Actually, quite a lot can be determined, as she well knew. Cars in the country were how you identified people. Get yourself a new vehicle and for days you'll go unacknowledged, suspected of being a stranger until someone winkles you out.

Minutes before, my cousin Nile had flashed past on the main road in his black Buick, heading deeper into the country, having bagged some willing-enough girl at a dance or the bowling alley. Even at that distance and with only the headlights to go by—the Buick's body smudged into the night—Mother knew who it was. She had to smile then, for somewhere along the line she had acquired a taste for bad news, the only kind Nile knew how to deliver. She'd consider the girl, silent in the seat beside him, a young body skin-tight with desire, and may have envied her. Short-lived envy. (I'm only guessing.)

Our road was a good half mile long, so she had plenty of opportunity to observe the car's progress, its steady creeping approach. She would have watched it turn, where Nile's car had not turned. She'd been expecting it—clearly—yet its appearance startled. It had broken into an atmosphere of expectation that had grown unreal. Her fear accelerated, or her excitement, depending. Ruling out Saturday night joyriders, her snooping family, vigilantes, and complete losers out tooling around, it had to be either him—or him.

What *was* it about her? On the whole, I was smarter, funnier, faster on my feet, and much better company. These are not attributes anyone should undervalue (I also had a sharp eye and packed a penknife), but those headlights were aimed directly at her. They were coming for her and I was powerless to stop them, being stopped myself, immobile as scenery, a dead weight sunk in unknowing.

During the civilized, waking hours, I'd been known to stand in front of the door, arms stretched wide, blocking her exit. The first time I tried this amused her, in a complicated sort of way, of which I hoped shame formed a large part. After I'd pulled this stunt a few more times, she was less amused, but the complication remained like a rat in my hair that wouldn't untangle.

"Hero, let me through. I'm going to town, all right? Shopping?"

"Can I come?"

"Sorry. Next time."

"There'll be one?"

"Of course."

"Where's Dad?"

"Having a nap, don't bother him."

"He's sad, I'll cheer him up."

"He's tired, leave him be."

"Are we getting our new house?"

"I don't know, now please *move*."

We needed a new house because she broke the old one trying to find her way out. No one needed a wrecking ball with her around—she was our very own Wonder Woman wrenching the panelling off the walls with her bare hands.

It didn't matter if she went to town without me. Not much. The empties were stored under the sink and it was more agreeable to take my time draining them. Healthier, too, seeing as I'd chugged a floating butt or two on more hurried raids. If allowed to go, I would have to be the anchor of the expedition, her parole officer, her personal scold—a glum functionary reminding her of what's what. There was always, *always* the chance that she wouldn't come back (and she hadn't said *which* town, had she?), but keep going on and on, exploring her own uncharted and expanding universe. We were never free of that possibility. I didn't see her as being overly useful or necessary to have around, but Father didn't need the grief.

"How could I have been so *bloody* stupid?" he had asked, dismayed. Indeed, looking as though he'd received a dunning blow to the head.

I knew a rhetorical question when I heard one, and so did she, incredibly. At least she had the good grace not to say, "Yes, how could you have been?"

I also knew that when your trust in someone doesn't work out, when it flips around and hits you in the face, it's called stupidity instead of good faith.

Father had been bilked by a contractor, a veritable city slicker, one part jester and two parts concentrated slime. He'd been taken to the cleaner's. The deal had been preceded by drinks, laughs, plans. The plans? The realization of my mother's dream home, but it was a very bad dream.

"A marble floor in the living room, would you like that?" Father slipped his arms around her. (How could he?)

"Morland," she laughed. "Marble?"

How many times did he want to be the town's laughingstock? *What's he trying to build her?* I overheard my grandmother muttering to herself. *A mausoleum?*

"Two limestone fireplaces, one in the living room and one down in the rec room."

Great. He could display his horns on one of the mantels.

"We'll need some new furniture, I suppose, but Morrie I don't see how we can. . . ."

A long, protest-stopping kiss. Disgusting. She was probably carrying a disease. A tapeworm that would slide out of her mouth into his, swim up to his brain, and tie it up in a fancy bow. A gift for the contractor.

The new house was to be built closer to town so that she wouldn't feel so isolated, so far from the hot hub and the gossipy goings-on that didn't remotely interest her. I knew she'd rather eat pins than go to a euchre party or attend a meeting of the Women's Institute. For this I couldn't blame her.

A real fishwife wouldn't speak, would she? Wouldn't give away her secrets, wouldn't know our language, a creature netted and pulled out of another element entirely.

She had a soft, young voice, honest and clean. She didn't nag, I'll say that for her. She seemed happy enough. So what was the problem? Why did she have to stand at the window and stare so hungrily and helplessly out, like some elderly soul whose life had vanished utterly?

She wouldn't know exactly who was driving down our road, which of the two, that was the thing.

Work on the new house stalled at the foundation, a giant's empty grave that filled up with darkness at night, or some scurrying, luckless animal that tumbled in. A mucky floor, piles of sand, ripped bags of cement, abandoned tools. Hard to imagine it turning into what Father had envisioned: a beautiful house, an enticing house, the envy of all. It was more like a failed fallout shelter.

A family on the other side of town hadn't gotten much further with their place, either. They ran out of money—or will—for they had slapped a tarpaper roof overtop of their concrete block walls and moved in, contentedly enough, or simply resigned to living in a hovel. Father always had to comment on it when we drove by, shaking his head, incredulous—"Look at that place, *look at it.*" But now he wasn't saying too much. He never seemed to sleep, but got into the car after supper and drove off.

The contractor sent us a box of presents from Mexico. A donkey piñata for me, a silver bracelet for Mother, a gay, wide-brimmed sombrero for Father. Embarrassed for us all, Mother chucked her bracelet into the lake.

Father believed in the blood warmth of a home. He could smell dinner cooking in the fancy new oven, saw me sailing across the marble floor in my sock feet, heard laughter not grounded in anything nasty. (Better not invite Aunt Faith over, then.) He dreamed of giving her a fabulous place—*Home & Garden* standard (skip the garden)—an interior so satisfying that she wouldn't need, or want, to go out. Ever. Wouldn't even put a foot out the door to see what the weather was like. But that other one, the man creeping down our road (it could be him) came from the outside, and was made of outside stuff, and had nothing at all to offer her except the *outside*.

"I honestly don't know what he'll do, if he finds him."

Unprecedented, Mother confiding in her sister-in-law, Auntie Viv. She was that desperate.

"Don't worry," said Auntie Viv. "He won't do a freakin' thing. That *scumbag* deserves to have the shit kicked out of him, mind."

"He's been gone for two whole days. That's not like him, he's *never* done that before."

I could almost hear Viv thinking, *So it's your turn, eh, sweetheart?* But having gained unprecedented access here, Viv knew better than to plug up this trickle of inside news with sarcasm or home truths.

"He'll kill him, that's what. He *will*, I know it."

"Morrie? Bah." Viv paused, doing some more thinking on the subject. The boyfriend had gotten away with it, and Cousin Tony had gotten away with it, and God knows who else, but apparently her brother had recently rediscovered the location of his balls and the contractor wasn't going to be so lucky. After all, losing a woman was one thing, but a bank account full of hard-earned cash was another more serious loss altogether. "Where's he keep his rifles, did ya say?"

Everyone hunts. Recreational killing, it's a rural thing. It's also convenient: when the McFarland's moved from their farm into town, they took the dogs out to the bush and shot them to save the trouble of taking them along. In the spirit of this, I whaled hell out of my piñata. I laid the donkey on the ground, smashed in its head with a rock, whacked it with a baseball bat, kicked it, gutted it. The candy that spilled out—a cardboard carcass hemorrhaging sweetness—I had no intention of throwing in the lake. I was determined to get *something* out of this deal, even if the candy had been licked by the lizard tongues of the Mexican children who had wrapped it so prettily in coloured cellophane.

Licked, spat on, or worse. Who cares, we had already been poisoned.

My room in the new house would have been painted pink, like the inside of a lung (a kid's lung). I wasn't crazy about this scheme, but I still wanted the room. I wanted to sit inside my room listening to records, listening to my digestion, listening to voices in the living room kept low because the subjects being discussed were humdrum and not worth getting worked up about.

Balancing on top of the cement foundation, one foot placed squarely in front of the other, I moved around and around the nonexistent house, pretending to be hazarding an endless tightrope walk. Gazing through the transparent walls, I could almost see us in there. With some effort, and some will. What were we doing? Swimming aimlessly, or floating on our backs, unmoored.

The tellers at the bank would have all seen the fat cheque Father wrote for the contractor, the flourish of his signature swirling a notch out of control after too much Crown Royal, the serif on the butt of his name wagging like a dog's tail. They probably passed the cheque around among themselves, eyebrows raised, lips pursed, no choice but to clear it. The money disappeared out of the account, out of our town, out of the country. Everyone knew. Tellers aren't called tellers for nothing. (I'm not the only one around with loose lips.) The money was meant to pay for lumber, windows, doors, nails, shingles, marble, brick, insulation, wiring, bathroom fixtures, tiles, Formica counters, drywall, appliances, paint. Undreamy materials, including the sucky pink. Work on the house stopped dead.

Whether or not the contractor had also been stopped dead was a question she must have been asking herself as she watched the headlights approach. If it was him returning. A fifty-fifty chance. Could be her husband, gripping the steering wheel hard to keep his hands from shaking. Driving slowly because he'd been into the Crown Royal again, this time for the courage to strike a different sort of bargain. Or he was driving slowly because he didn't want to arrive. Ever. As he neared the house, he would see only her silhouette as she stood at the picture window gazing out, a dark, flat, featureless woman. His shadow-wife, the ideal occupant of a never-never house.

So *was* it my father returning with another man's blood on his hands, or was it another man, blood intact and piping hot, coming to get her? This man would at least be able to offer her a different form of humiliation. A house with a sickening roominess, the walls always receding, but the enclosure unmistakable.

I pictured Grendel's own mother snatching up the silver bracelet from the bottom of the lake and slipping it onto her green wrist. Told you I was smart. Although I didn't want to know everything.

Tormented by uncertainty, bound by it, she would not have been able to move from her place at the glass. She was fixed in her steady surveillance. But I couldn't stand it, the unsettling house rumours had reached me, tweaking the bedcovers, pinching, pulling at my arms. Up, *up*. The curtains in my room were like reeds I swept aside, my window opened to the night. The long grass against my legs was wet with snake spit, the stones on the shore were cold underfoot, and smooth. I didn't slip, but moved steadily on and away, whisper-quick. The leeches were dimly aware of me, the caddis worms, the crayfish, I was the brief tremor on their rooftops, a shudder of fear passing.

And on the road, the car moving like a dream toward the house, moving soundlessly, weighted with the unspeakable, a wraith of dust trailing behind, its driver and deliverer no concern of mine.

# Far Cry

My mother played bridge—we all knew what that meant—and my grandmother had a bridge in her mouth, an otherworldly conveyance, a feat of engineering that repeatedly secured my escape. Just so you know, I wasn't some lamebrained kid, but a linguistic opportunist. I fashioned my own understanding of what this bridge was for. Not, *Oh-my-grandmother, what-big-teeth-you-have.* No, this was not about choppers that were gross and even bigger (and *grosser)* when submerged and magnified in a glass of water resting on her nightstand. More this: open your mouth Grams, tell me a tale and I'm gone, self dissolved, bodiless surfing on an ethereal plane.

Not so for her, though. Her own life had begun to resemble a house in which more and more of the rooms were closing up. What remained in this equivalence of life = house? The kitchen, the porch, one crammed closet, a guest bedroom (she was the guest), and a small dark room at the very back that she could enter if she so wished. She did not wish. Her dead husband crouched there, waiting. The *memory* of him, mind, this is not some freezer story. She'd seen him enough in life and didn't feel the need to refresh her own memory with a visit to the small dark room. But it was there, unlocked and available, unlike so many of the other rooms that had once constituted her life.

This may have been why she decided to build a shed. No metaphor this, but a real shed.

She already had one that housed the lawnmower, the snow shovels, the gardening tools, and the other practical outdoor paraphernalia. So a new shed for… who could say, she'd figure that out after it was built. Albertha liked the feel of fresh lumber in her hands almost as much as she liked gazing into a clean, empty bowl. Both served up potential, the provender of the possible.

Plans were drawn up at the kitchen table: exactitude has its joys. She twirled the pencil in her fingers, ran a thumb along the dental strafing her daughter had once given it. In grade school the girl had chewed her pencils so fiercely that the metal ends were mashed flat. The gnawed-off erasers had spent more time trekking through her digestive tract than they had rubbing out her many mistakes. Perhaps they had erased something essential during their fantastic voyage through her insides, something a nice girl needs. Considering what my mother later got up to, her savaged pencils were doubtless overlooked tools for personality assessment and prognostication. As a child, her mildness and compliance had concealed traits more socially acidic than anyone would have guessed. Teething never ends for some.

You didn't have to explain to anyone why you needed a shed, or two for that matter. Equipment accrued, ditto sacks of seed, cement, rat poison, tar, wood for the stove, solvents, machinery all sizes, stacks of empty apple-baskets, lawn chairs, yard sale do-dads, useless stuff exiled from the house. *Et cetera* without end.

Albertha drove the truck to town, a beer tucked between her legs for the ride. The cop she passed on the way, and with whom she exchanged a two-finger wave, did likewise. She stopped at the lumber yard, then the hardware store, allowing the town's knowledge of the shed's existence to precede the actuality of the shed itself. A bee that consisted solely of buzz. Altogether she bought tongue-and-groove pine, plywood, a tri-angle vent, cedar shingles, soffits, two kinds of nails, stain (with a hint of blue in it), a door, and… glass. She wanted her shed to have a window. This raised a few eyebrows, but they settled down comfortably enough. A woman's fixture, a window. Otherwise where would she put the curtains?

Albertha knew, of course, that there are occur-rences entirely possible that fall within the realm of fantasy. She might win a lottery; she might learn to speak Mandarin; her daughter might decide to act like a proper married woman and not some horny ado-lescent. But she doubted it. On the other hand, she might *really* build a church, a shed of worship with a congregation of one. If she were inclined in that direction. Hardly the case. She figured that the Man Above already had His gnarled arthritic fingers stuck in enough earthly real estate. Could be God *was* real estate. If she wanted a building for the purpose of developing her spiritual side, there'd be no one to stop her from dragging a mat out to the shed and setting it up for meditation. Or yoga. (Corpse position, no rush.) Who knows, she might even get her head together like her neighbour Ray's son did, or aimed to do, by hitchhiking out West and not returning until Ray's own head was slowly coming apart underground. The boy had inherited the Doan homestead, one fallow field away—fallow except for the burdock, vetch, fleabane, ragweed, and lamb's quarters. Kim Doan hadn't sold up as expected, but continued to live there, presumably engaged in some pursuit other than sending corkscrews of cannabis smoke twirling through the cracks in the windows. As far as Albertha could tell, the only thing holding Kim's head together these days was a tightly cinched ponytail.

She tried not to hurry it, took it step by measured step. Once the gravel had been delivered—and a load of bullshit with it—she chose the site, backyard near the spruce, as far as possible from the house. As one day latched onto the next, she dug a base, packed in the gravel, levelled the skids, assembled the floor, raised the walls, installed the roof framing, shingles, siding, door, window, hardware. At night she dreamed it out of the ground, walls alive, moonlight-thin, a faintly shimmering blue, more ball gown than shed. All told, the indulgence of constructing it, roofing it, staining it, proceeded like a dream. Not a single hitch slowed her down. Especially not the insignificant hurts that were part of the process, the slivers, the skinned knuckle, the barked and bruised knee. Finished, it shone with her pleasure and satisfaction. The oiled and squeakless hinges were as bright as gold; the doorknob, breeze-buffed, a cool thrill to twist. Her creation was unpretentious and handsome, herself as architecture, built to last.

Ray, her old neighbour, would have admired her handiwork, and her husband, old what's-his-name, would not have. Her bookends, her male brackets. Not that the opinions of the dead pertained. Forget them, she had a shed for shouting in. Not that she had anything to shout about outside of the shed itself. Fine then, a shed for silliness: she could fill it to the brim with acorns, or cabbages, (no kings). She could torch it and keep its ashes in a jar under her bed. Although she didn't think that having endured the privations of the Depression, the War, motherhood, and widowhood, granted her the mad luxury of doing something so wasteful and pointless. Her amateur theatre for bad ideas, then. How about nabbing herself a hostage, for the hell of it, no one would ever guess. That young English teacher from the high school, say. The one who taunted the girls—certain girls—with what they would never attain, but also never forget.

English teachers can be a bloody nuisance. She'd have to remember to warn Hero (that's me!).

Her short, uncombed hair stood up in front, a quiff of white; her unharnessed breasts did not. *Yeah, yeah.* She shrugged off the compressing expectations that came with her age and stepped into her newly risen shed, unencumbered. And as yet unencumbered with any true idea of what to do with it.

She had killed her husband, naturally. That's how she viewed it. The power of the spoken word. A confessional then? She shrugged this off, too. Didn't a confessional imply guilt or contrition? It hadn't been a shrivelling, black-hearted curse that had finished him off, nothing premeditated. And if anyone had an evil eye—or tongue—it had been him.

Albertha surveyed the interior, which was perfect, and breathed in the leftover sawdust smell, the raw wood, the stain, the latex paint, the nostril-tweaking vinegar fumes from the cleaned and newsprint-polished window. (Rubbed some slithering politician's face on it, making him do honest work for a change.) Her beautiful and precisely hung window. She smiled to think of the Bedard brothers from down the road, 'redecorating.' They'd painted right overtop the dead flies and wasps on the sills because they couldn't be bothered brushing them off. Or, more likely, it hadn't occurred to them to do so. Following this same logic of convenience, they'd recently dragged some dozen or so chickens into their living room to slaughter them, figuring it would be easier to do the job there. Men had different ideas of what a home was for.

She awarded herself a good long congratulatory look through her new window. Her gaze lighted across a field that used to be planted with corn one year, beans the next. Beans were better for keeping an eye on Ray, but a field of corn you could get lost in. Her gaze lingered on a clump of jail-break phlox, circled a granite boulder that had ancient squatting rights—too venerable to be routed—skimmed like a dragonfly over the split-rail fence, and landed on a decrepit Chevy Impala pulling into the Doan's driveway. Ray's old car. She realized then that what she had here was not so much a vista, a frame for the greenery, the sky, a solitude-puncturing hole on the world, as a one-program TV station starring

Kim Doan. (Give a boy a girl's name and no wonder he can't get his head together.) Curtains might be called for after all.

She wouldn't have minded seeing Ray step out of that car, but instead got the default option. Ray decomposing probably looked better than his son did now. Kim, skinny and skittish, whittled to premature middle-age, but dressed like a kid in cuffed jeans and a *HAIR* T-shirt (not the penitential kind). Arrested development in more ways than one. A wonder, frankly, that he managed to lug such a big case of beer into the house.

Albertha stepped back from the window, did a turn in her studio, her study, her undefined space. Her thought bubble filled with oxygen. Philosopher's shack, kitchen sink school. Institution of lower learning. Oldster's playhouse.

Heartbreak hotel.

A writing room? But then, hadn't she read recently that no one lives in the country anymore. No one worth writing about, that is, only bumpkin zombies in plush vests picking the corn out of their teeth with screwdrivers. Aesthetics, style, eloquence... can't keep that down on the farm. Edgy rural fiction, not a chance. Forget it then.

A waiting room.

She patted the wall, considered the floor. She *could* bring an armchair out, a carpet, footstool, some magazines, a bottle of whisky. Her reading days weren't over—horrible thought!—but they had been sorely filled. She had read and read and read to her dying husband. He had taken to books in his illness, although not to any other never-too-late passions that might have helped them both.

He had claimed that his eyes were failing him, although when reading to him they fastened on her as sharply as they had ever done. (The only failure evident in them, she suspected, was her.) Green eyes, heart-stopping embedded in a young man's face, and heart-stopping in an old one, but for different reasons.

Middle of the night—any time she was in the middle of *anything*—she'd hear him call from the downstairs sitting room where she'd set up his sick bed. He made a sound like a baby, a distant but piercing wail that hooked directly into her middle and made her jump. He needed another hit of morphine, followed-up by another flank of words to suck some life from. Literature as transfusion. Not that he'd tolerate the words that any living writer had pulled together; he wanted to hear the voices of the dead. Dead but still lucent: Dickens, Hardy, Thackeray.

"Joyce?" she'd asked once, brandishing a volume of stories snatched up from a box of books their daughter had dropped off.

"No damn females," he rasped back.

A childish trick, but she'd enjoyed it.

"Trollope?" she said.

He glared at her.

Not that Albertha minded the chore. Much better than sitting by listening to his breath guttering out, the wrenching exorcism of what remained. She had a flair for reading aloud. Her voice soft where required, or soaring, expressive, dramatic, but never soppy, never slipping into a bog of sentiment. She meant every word, she got involved. He watched her intently during the whole performance. Did he listen? She wondered. This verbal medicine may simply have been a substitute for something else unrendered over the years.

They *did* have years banked, not all bad.

There were times, true, when she had refused to open her mouth at all because her tongue felt burned, blackened with some news from the outer world she couldn't bring herself to deliver.

She heard a noise, someone calling. Company? Somebody dropping by to check out the shed? *Spare me.* They'd come soon enough, and her land art (so there!) would have to revert momentarily to what it wasn't: a utility shed. Whereas a livelier eye might see a retirement home for skunks, an ant mansion, a B&B for Martians. Who's to say? In essence, it was one big uncrackable naught. (And *not* symbolic. Leave that for English class. I stood warned.) Why else call it a shed if definition didn't run off it like rain?

Not near, that noise. Albertha glanced out the window, let her look stray across the way again (habit), and damned if she didn't see her own daughter striding up the Doan's driveway, pushing her flash new bicycle, calling Kim's name, her tone gay and reckless. She propped her bike against the side of the house, calling louder, shameless, letting everyone in the township know her whereabouts *and* her intentions. She scampered up the back steps like a squirrel, a pretty squirrel, and let herself in without knocking. Her bike fell over, clattered to the ground. Careless.

If confronted, Albertha knew, word for word, what her daughter would say: *Christ, mother, we're friends! I've known Kim since forever, haven't I? Remember? Get a grip.*

Get a grip? In lieu of a handsome silk tie, Albertha supposed her daughter would have to get a grip on that ponytail of his, yank him this way and that, bring him to his knees, flip up her skirt. With any luck, she'd jump on the worthless bastard and flatten him.

He'd wounded his dad. Ray had longed to hear from him, a word or two would have done. He pined for the boy. People had to stop asking about him. There'd been no cause for the silence that she knew of. Ray hadn't been the kind to lay a hand on him and the mother had been decent enough while she was around. His son had never caught them—Albertha and Ray—rolling around on crushed cornstalks in the middle of the field, because it had never happened. Sometimes Ray would give her a shout and a wave from his tractor, but that wasn't the dictionary definition of infidelity. (Dignity in distance, right?) Not that she could have convinced her husband otherwise. Not that she tried. He had some grievance against their neighbour in any case, involving land and fences, a perceived wrong that he'd nursed until he had made something palpable and irrefutable of it.

He could easily build something out of nothing, although nothing you'd want to take shelter in.

How do you deny that you're not involved in a wrong without sounding like you are? And if you're simply thinking about it, then you're equally guilty. No, no confessional for her.

Her daughter had slipped almost effortlessly out of Albertha's body, slick as a little animal, and as a soapy baby in the bath had slipped squirming and giggling out of her hands, and now, lithe and smooth-skinned, had slipped with ease into Kim Doan's arms. Who was the careless one?

For a time, life burned in two pairs of eyes, one reading, one watching. She sometimes wondered if he were trying to take her with him and the ongoing sentences were the link, the cord he'd use to tug her through, headfirst into oblivion. A strand of understanding did seem at times to stretch between them, although one fabricated by others.

One night she tried extemporizing. She wandered off the page's margin and away, filling in boldly with a line or two of her own, then more and more brazenly, a story beginning to build about he and she and him, but he caught her out. (No Joyce she, no Michael Furey resurrected in a pronoun.) He *had* been listening. He grunted, surprised and annoyed, and so, before he got into it, she picked up where she'd left off, toed the line as written. But he wasn't satisfied: she'd ruined it. He made a choking noise, a series of choking noises, ugly, desperate sounds. His fury wordless, but fully expressed. Exhausted, sleep-deprived but not sorrow-deprived, she snapped the book shut. She raised her head to glare back at him, to challenge him—she controlled this show after all—and saw that he was looking straight through her. Green eyes, heart-stopping in a dead man. After weeks and weeks, he'd heard enough, or had enough. Had enough of her certainly, but it felt like unfinished business all the same. No ending, she couldn't bear to reopen that book.

When she stepped out of the shed—spy sanctuary, hidey-hole—Albertha looked askance at the back of the house where the small dark room would be if the small dark room were real, if there *were* a bridge that one could cross from the known to the unknown.

Whatever her shed's function might be, it took up a fact's worth of space. It stood solid and grounded, enclosing a silence.

So consider this, Hero: Rely on a bridge made of words and odds are you'll eventually fall to your death.

# Unwhisperable

Our house not only magnified sound, but translated it, added a spin to it, juiced it up for effect. Call it a storey-teller. This had much to do with the resonance of hardwood, the layout, and malicious acoustics. So you had Father cracking leftover Christmas walnuts in the kitchen and me upstairs hearing him crack open skulls—leftovers from some war other than the annual tinselly one. How could it not catch my attention, this bone-crunching and splintering racket, left lobe collapsing into right— logic veering recklessly into creativity—nut meats exposed? Precisely the sort of thing I was after: booty from the interior.

However, descent into the kitchen would only bring disappointment. When had it ever brought anything else? Except toast. A man standing with his gut pressed lightly into the aluminum edge of the counter, wearing new, airmail blue, still-creased from the package Christmas boxers, chewing contemplatively as he stares out of a window as unrevealing as a night-black stamp, before him an absurdly high mound of walnut shells, irreparably broken, while the house remains intact, but groans and creaks and carries on from the effort.

I couldn't go down to check anyway, as my curiosity was reputedly in remission.

Having spent a tad too much time looking for trouble, and succeeding in the quest, the household authorities had strongly advised a hobby. Which is why I was spending this precious, yet too-slowly dissolving evening of my life rustling through a five-and-dime store package of stamps, a starter philately set, trying to work up... what? Enthusiasm? Far too much to hope for. Likewise tepid interest, or mildly asphyxiating boredom. The diversion at hand appeared only to be diverting me into a mood disorder, dragging my robust personality over the borderline. Basically, my efforts were concentrated on not slitting my wrists and bleeding all over the Queen's face or on any other worldly postage-worthy icon. What I really wanted was to read the letters onto which these paper scraps had once been affixed. I would have liked that *very* much, regardless of the quality of the contents. I wanted news of the world, the inner world of who thought what, and who did what to whom, and how much it hurt, and what happened then.

Not that I needed letters generally. Walls had ears, and ours had ears as big as laundry chutes. Confidential information whispered in an upstairs room reliably resulted in a dump of dirty laundry at your feet. I may not have collected much dirt from the clandestine goings-on in Malaysia or Hong Kong, but I had acquired a respectable heap of the local product. I offer here some samples from my varied collection.

My Aunt Faith. You'd never guess to look at her that she, rigid of mind and body, had an outward bound uterus whenever she sneezed. How she coaxed it back into place had yet to be disclosed, as this is not the sort of slippage a woman wants to discuss with anyone, including herself. Theoretically, and if only out of self-interest, knowledge of the infirmities of others should make us more sympathetic, but in Aunt Faith's case, I was all for presenting her with bouquets of ragweed or gift bags bulging with particulate matter. In my view, her tongue, and possibly her soul, needed that pessary far more. Beyond the subject of her restless maternal organ, she was not shy about confiding to anyone who would listen the details of her recent near-death and out-of-body experience.

Two months back, she slipped on the stairs at her place and down she went. On the way, she not only saw the Lord, but He caught her essential self in His arms, while they both watched her material self roll like a log to the bottom. Thereafter she claimed Him to be, not only *The* Saviour, but her personal saviour.

(The Lord, I'd begun to notice, no longer operated as much by stealth as He had once done. Not only that but He had enlisted an expanding and highly annoying PR team. Get this, I buy a bag of wax lips from Park's Variety and Mrs. Park, a grown woman, tells me about being so exhausted the night before that she barely got her prayers said before falling asleep. I care? Sly proselytizing, that's all.)

(Good chance Mrs. Park has a disease more degenerative than religion that's making her tired. I'll enquire, delicately, tease her hidden ailment out, although physical failings aren't my main area of interest.)

Faith's fall was said to be my cousin Nile's fault. He'd left an empty on the top step, or at least didn't claim otherwise, didn't try to shift the blame onto his dad. Nile didn't give a shit, not then or at an age usually described as tender. Made of tough stuff, he'd entered the world as hardtack, Teflon-coated, and no wonder, his mother apparently indestructible. She came to at the bottom of the stairs, reborn, and with a bonus set of saucepan-sized bruises on her rear. The Lord's thumb prints.

According to my Auntie Viv, Faith herself was as drunk as a lord at the time (the only lord in attendance) and being too blotto to break any bones, she bounced, rubberized, the entire way down. She'd likely left the empty on the step in the first place, letting Nile take the blame, plus a crack on the head. He didn't care. If his mother had died in the fall, whether he cared or not would have been his to know. But, seeing as Faith got reborn out of the deal, the crack on the head was probably more for show. They smacked each other around on a regular basis, there being a kind of dumb-show vocabulary to it.

Faith's story has its moments (quick ones), but Viv's no fool. She knows what she's talking about, being a drinker herself, although not a secret one. Viv had too much obvious fun for that, and in any event was a socialist when it came to classified information. She believed in sharing the wealth. Anyhow, if that's all there was to it, if booze had become Faith's private vice and inspirational source, it's hardly worth mentioning. Some hushed-up transgressions in town were of a similar order—commonplace, garden-variety, low-wattage sins. The only embarrassment occasioned by their discovery would derive from their inferior quality; the only way of keeping their inherently dull power intact would be to keep mum. Low interest being better than none.

"Mrs. Park has a problem with her head," I confided to Auntie Viv, curious to see how this might play. "Not anything serious, I don't think." Sometimes one has to be proactive, even with the truth.

"You don't say."

Having been shortchanged on more than one occasion at Park's, Viv must have felt she had proof enough. The story went around and came back as a sizable malignant tumour. My community is nothing if not caring.

Viv had the right idea. Secrets can be corrosive. Better out than in. If Mrs. Park hadn't been so dutifully repressing her anger under a thick blanket of prayer laid down night after night, she wouldn't have gotten so sick in the first place. When soon afterward I stopped by Park's for some jawbreakers, it gratified me to hear her suppressing her anger a whole lot less, and for that I should be commended.

I had to wonder if her husband beats her, too? Looks the type.

Some people do harm themselves over the most piddling of unforgettable misdeeds. Guilt or regret can whet to an eviscerating sharpness, indiscretions, or stupid mistakes or impulsive, uncharacteristic behaviours. Like our principal, Mr. Morris, swiping a lipstick (*Cherries in the Snow*) out of Batty Pock's purse after she excused herself (diarrhea) during an interview about what her son did with that dog. (The things that go on!) Or like Gloria Kay telling her elderly dad after he wet himself that he made her, "*sick sick sick*." Experiencing a bout of PMS at the time, and having that very day drained the old man's bank account, Gloria never entirely forgave herself for misspeaking. (His black eye came later.)

And, getting back to the subject of tumours, I know without a doubt that some people carried dead weights within them that slowed their stride, but quickened their hearts unhealthily with the burden. Jane Miller's furtive abortion; Francine Smith's drug problem; Tommy Lean's sneak affair with his wife's sister that led to divorce and remarriage with the sister and an empty church on one side at the wedding, plus the very same devil of a mother-in-law and a festering load of misery because the second sister turned out to be more maritally chilly than the first. You'd think a dentist wouldn't be so hasty. (For fact-checking, their phone numbers are all in the book.)

Before he croaked, rashly and unexpectedly, I used to visit Grandfather Young in the old age home, a harshly lit institution softened for its residents by their deteriorating eyesight and their withdrawal from expectation. Here, it was almost too easy, like picking windfalls after a storm. The storm being in this case the final blast of life itself loosening and unravelling the bindings of propriety and discretion. Perversities, intolerances, cruelties—the residents let fly long-held tidbits. The aged divulged seasoned secrets without batting an eye, and whether some did so knowingly under the forgiving shelter of dementia, I, for one, was not about to smoke them out.

Grandfather Young, a soft-spoken man, generous and personable, had more liberal views than most of his contemporaries, and I'd never heard him denigrate others for any reason. So imagine my surprise when I entered his room one day and heard, "Get out of here you black bastard!" This he addressed to the West Indian doctor who had kindly stopped by at the request of a vacationing (gambling, not golfing) Doc McIvor.

"Grandad!"

The man didn't linger, but took the hit in a manly enough way. God knows, he must have been used to it, although in town racist remarks were usually delivered more thoughtfully. Had Grandfather picked it up out of the air, all those old brains leaking malice, or was some long buried rot beginning to surface? Or was he simply having some nasty fun?

"*You're* a bastard," he said.

"I am not."

"Your mother's a tramp."

"Okay, that's it, Grandad. I'm out of here."

"Don't go, Hero."

"Don't be mean, then."

"You still diddling that cousin of yours?"

"I'm only a kid! *Jesus.*"

There *had* been some hanky-panky, true, but that was my business.

"Girls. All whores."

"That's it, I'm leaving. See you around." I stood to go.

"Wait, wait. You want to hear what Osbert Kay's been saying about his daughter, don't you?"

"Yeah, maybe." I resumed my seat, primly. "But listen Grandad, you better watch what you say. You know, in that doctor's *black* bag there are needles."

For the record, Nile and I had this game that had been going on for some time, innocent enough. He'd undress me, slowly, slowly, then when stripped clean, he'd run his hands all over me, up and down, legs and feet, back and neck, chest and belly, not an inch of my bod exempt. Talk about sensitive material! But that's all there was to it, not like that business he got up to with some of the older girls. The whole deal friendly and harmless, a familiarity among the related, a feel-good family event. Unfortunately, my house had treachery built into its framework. Try to have some kind of fun behind closed doors and sure enough one of those doors would pop open at the exactly the wrong moment. With one's mother standing on the threshold, aghast.

She should talk.

I wish she would, for there was something, *something* not right. When my parents were out, I cruised through the house searching for it, busy little fingers unlocking and opening and prying loose. You'd think the place would cooperate, but squeaking cupboards do not translate. What I found in the medicine cabinet only told me that among us we suffered from headaches, constipation, colds, gingivitis (who wanted to go to a dentist who'd screwed his wife's sister?), cuts, warts, indigestion, car sickness (guess who?), depression, watery eyes, insomnia, and hemorrhoids. Commonplace afflictions. But I knew that a more grievous one, an affliction that caused uncommon pain had been secreted somewhere in the house. Like a lost key, it was unreachable for having fallen through a crack invisible to me.

When people smile at you with pity, or smirk with the pleasurable pressure on their lips that withholding knowledge about you causes, you understand that it's an open secret. Everyone knows but you, so they're making some nominal effort to protect you—while letting you know it—but mostly they're keeping themselves entertained. I don't think this thing involves my father, or not directly. He may have hurt a man who cheated him once, and I don't know how badly, but that really is a family secret, scabbed over and untouched, not picked at by anyone, including me.

That leaves my mother. She could whip up a batch of shame faster than most mothers can make a cake. What had she been up to now? Lips were sealed (mostly with other lips, but that's another story). Including Auntie Viv's, which did not bode well. She fobbed me off with a questionable cliché, "What you don't know won't hurt you, eh." Plus a glass of doctored O.J. that had a real kick to it. An aid to Viv saying, "Forget it, Hero."

So.

"What's up?" I asked Nile, a generation older than me and packed solid with knowing.

"Let's play our game and see."

"Not allowed, remember."

"All the better."

"People are *thinking* things about me. Tell me."

"Poor baby." Before undoing the top button of my shirt, he picked up a strand of my black hair and rolled it between his fingers, as if assessing its worth. "Who's your daddy?"

Here I thought this a trifling question. Impish, if formulaic. No response required. Seems I was wrong.

You see, for all my searching, the answer wasn't in the house after all. It was in me. Philately turns out to be the appropriate punishment for my curiosity because I myself bear a stamp. My mother, clever woman, had concealed it in a place I'd never think to look. But I did. This, a covert operation performed without anaesthesia. I had to reach in and claw it out. Had to bloody my hand digging into my own heart.

Who did what to whom? How much did it hurt? Who's my daddy?

# Small Talk

My father's philosophical musings were often hybrid affairs—a marriage of pseudo-Confucian sayings, popular proverbs, and original material—that required a sharp instrument, a kind of analytical nut-pick, to extract from them their meaty flecks of wisdom. My mother and I, enjoying at his expense a rare phase of solidarity, referred to these utterances as "according to Confusion" or "what Confusion say."

"Pithy," she'd observe.

"*Pithy*," I'd agree.

And then we'd laugh.

The 'He-who's' didn't always lead to 'hee-haws,' however, and when trouble began to brew I headed out the door.

"Can't you get anything right, Morrie?" Arms crossed, toe tapping, classic signs. "He who hesitates is *lost*. Not 'laughing.' *Lost*. You know, like HE WHO hesitated to apply for that job at the dairy, or HE WHO didn't quite get around to. . . ."

As Ovid says, "Love is a kind of warfare." Or conversely, Molière: "Tranquility in love is a disagreeable calm." Whatever Confusion had to say on the subject would not, I feared, resolve the issue, so when battle lines were drawn I left them to it.

On one such auspicious day, far more thunder within than without, I set off to make my rounds. First, this involved a minor detour. In need of sustenance ("One cannot think well, love well, sleep well, if one has not dined well"—trust Virginia Woolf to nail it), and having secured an unofficial loan from the parents' modest savings ill-concealed in a locked strong box hidden beneath a floorboard upon which sat a hefty chest of drawers, I set out for Park's Variety. Mrs. Park's son, Rodney, a contemporary of mine, stood behind the cash, inert despite the surge of testosterone coursing through his male byways on seeing me enter.

"Rodney."

"Hero."

I mooched around in the store poking at cellophane wrappers and sliding open the freezer's glass panel, liberating the frost spirits trapped within. At some future date I'd have to sue the Park's for extreme dental distress, but at present was mightily pleased with the sugary wares on offer: jawbreakers, sponge toffee, Lucky Elephant Pink Candy Popcorn, Dixie cups, Licorice Cigars… *et cetera* was never so sweet. I settled on a cherry popsicle and dug in my pocket for a nickel. When I held it out to Rodney, he didn't budge. He stood motionless, staring at me, jeopardizing our commercial transaction.

"Five cents, right?" Sometimes one had to give Rodney a wee prompt, get the show on the road.

He continued to stare, utterly immobile.

I knew he was alive, knocking around in there somewhere. "Yoo-hoo, Rodney. Anyone home?"

"Your lips," he said.

"My—?"

Were they scaly, or something? Had I inadvertently broken out in melanotic maculae, cankers, Kawasaki syndrome? I hadn't checked when I got up that morning. (Indeed, I don't believe I'd washed.) I prided myself on not wearing makeup, letting my natural charms do all the work required. In error, perhaps? No one had ever mentioned my lips before, except to comment that I "flapped" them too much.

"What about them?"

"They're the same as your cousin's."

"Amy's?" Big-hipped, thin-lipped Amy? The suggestion brought my own bottom lip perilously close to quivering.

"*No.* Nile's. Same upper lip, same lower, same commissure, same vermilion border, same philtrum even. Don't you know that?"

Who else but Rodney would know the parts of the mouth? But *crap*, I realized it was true. If Nile ever uncurled his kisser from that Elvis sneer, it'd be a perfect match with mine. *All* our parts probably matched! (To wit, in the appropriate gendered arrangement, inappropriately paired.)

"So?" I said.

He shrugged, then stuck out his hand for payment.

I slapped the popsicle into his palm. "Break this, will you."

Rodney smacked it on the edge of the counter, handed it back, and rang in the sale.

"See ya." I pushed through the door.

"Yup."

Well, that was diverting. I slid the first half of the popsicle out of the package, stuck it in my mouth, and, with a vampiric focus, began to drain it of red dye # 40 as I took yet another slight detour. This one enabled me to start at the top of Ballentine, our one affluent street, as I made my way downtown, savouring my breakfast while enjoying a round of homegrown tourism. (Most of us lived on the other side of the tracks. In my family's case, we lived so far on the other side we couldn't even see the tracks.) The houses here were all larger than the ones on the other streets—fancier, impeccably maintained, heart-ache-free. You understood that their interiors would be as tastefully appointed and immaculate as their weedless and selectively treed yards. (Ah, the gingko, the tulip tree.) Somehow I couldn't envision tangled tumbleweeds of dust and hair rolling down the residents' long hard-wood-floored hallways (waxed to a high shine), nor picture anonymous pets skittering (slithering or hopping) terrified and squealing into holes gnawed in the wall (no holes!) should a confused child step on one at night in the unrelenting dark due to a misunderstanding over the hydro bill. Wandering down Ballentine, soothed by the street's funeral calm, and barely resisting the invitation to deposit my licked-clean popsicle stick on the out-stretched, albeit, lamp-holding hand of a lawn jockey, I considered Corbusier's assertion that, "A house is a machine for living in." I have to admit that this was not entirely comforting, as it sounded more like a device that might mill you into sawdust. Nevertheless, Hero, one of these days, one of these days…

On arriving in the business section, I finished off the second half of my popsicle, tucked both sticks in my shirtfront pocket, and stepped smartly into Pock's, which sold knickknacks, souvenirs, jewellery, and, for my purposes, comics. Judy, the Pock's oldest daughter, armed with nothing more welcoming than a worn-out feather duster and an exhausted expression, stood by a glass case filled with knockoff Royal Doulton figurines, the ladies within, despite their inferior porcelain pedigree, all demanding attention.

"'Lo, Judy."

"Mph."

She gave me a 'look,' but I didn't take it personally. The look was composed of many querulous ingredients: Why don't *you* have a job? (good question) Who do *you* think you are? (absurd question) Have you seen Nile around? (no) *You're* here to swipe something, aren't you? (who, *moi?*)

Did she voice aloud any of these questions to which she knew the answers? Her answers? No, instead we have—

"What's wrong with your *mouth?*"

Seemed to me people had been asking me that all my life, but it still caught me off guard. What *was* it with my mouth today? Had I fallen out of bed this morning transformed into Miss Potato Head, all my features scrambled?

She stepped closer, nostrils twitching, eyes narrowing. "Is it lipstick? Better get a few lessons on how to apply it."

Right, got it. I'd not only criminally breached my 'vermilion border,' but had jazzed up its youthful healthy hue with cherry popsicle. Not worth the effort of responding, I moved over to the rack of comics and gave it a dust-dispelling spin. Some of my favourites whirled by: *Caspar the Friendly Ghost, Richie Rich, Archie.*

"Don't *do* that, you'll break it."

Gave'er another spin, and this time it's, "Aren't you too *old* for comics?"

"Research."

"Yeah, yeah. Talking big again, Hero?"

*Thinking* big the appropriate response, but instead of continuing our cordial chat, I decided to put a plug in it. Conversation-wise, you couldn't find a better sink-stopper than the guy currently romancing Judy— one who'd already made the rounds with all the other older girls in town.

"So," I said. "How's Douggie doing?"

(Hark, did I hear the last lamenting gurgle of a drain?)

"That piece of shit? Who cares."

And off she went to the back of the store, blown by the self-generating winds of ill-will and frustration, leaving me to flip through the newest issues. I *was* doing research, too. In order to restore the family fortunes, I'd come up with the idea of writing a comic series of my own: *Molly Colossus, Adventures of a BIG Girl.* Picture it, Molly gets into some majorly tight spots, no end of thrills and chills, lots with physiological action sequences involving curled lips, crawling skin, and rolling eyes. I *had* considered calling the first issue 'Tight Spots,' but changed my mind in case it sounded too dermatologically painful. No want of material anyway, all I had to do was learn how to draw. In aid of this I'd sent away for a Jon Gnagy artist's kit that I'd seen advertised on TV before the tube burned out. This, the reason that my next destination was the post office, while seriously tempted to drop into the Red & White to take inventory, as it were, in a less well-travelled aisle.

No time to waste, I cast a farewell glance at Judy—as Confusion says, *"arse longa, vita brevis"*—and headed out.

Because my family moved so often, in town or out, or because my family was simply what it was (don't ask), we picked up our mail at the general delivery counter. Every day as I passed by the wall of postal boxes in the P.O.'s foyer, I paused momentarily, ardently wishing for a little silver key that would unlock our very own box. I knew that those boxes contained communications of a superior quality, unexpected bequests, news like no other, high-octane secrets unavailable anywhere else. And yet, if that were so, if that's where our mail nested, I'd miss out on talking with Mrs. Percy, the postmistress, who for some reason seemed concerned about my welfare.

"*More* bills today, Hero." She arrayed a stack of them on the counter, regretfully, as if having dealt out a particularly ruinous poker hand.

Bills, bills, bills. No matter, we had a special place for those at home. It's called a garbage can.

"Anything else, Mrs. Percy?" I swept up the bills and filed them in various pockets.

"Postcard from your Aunt Faith. Picture of kittens on the front. Heavens, I didn't know there was such a thing as an ugly kitten, but *my* these ones are real humdingers. Your aunt's away, is she?"

"She's *not*." Aunt Faith lived within spitting distance of us, stuck to her house like wallpaper. Although we *did* spot her yesterday coming up the drive, at which point we all hit the dirt—not necessarily a figurative expression at our place. "What's it say?"

Mrs. Percy made a show of turning the card over, but naturally she'd already read it. No point in working for the post office if you didn't keep your eye on community concerns. "A fool's mouth is his destruction. Proverbs 18:9."

Here we go again! *Geez.* "Can you send it back? You know, like in the song… '*Return to senderrrr, address unknooown—*'"

"'*No such numberrrr, no such zooone*'… Sure can. Your parents on the move again, dear?"

"No, no. A good spot, we're pretty settled. I love my room." The less said, the better. To resort to an old chestnut.

"There's no place like home."

I'm afraid this particular chestnut can be interpreted less positively, but I smiled and nodded, fashioning an agreeable expression that would also serve to hide my disappointment about the Learn to Draw Set. Jon Gnagy seemed like a very nice man and I had confidence that he wouldn't bilk my parents of their as yet unknown investment. Fair enough, no big deal, there's always tomorrow and tomorrow for the execution of those cubes and cones, their smudgy shadows falling every which way, defying the laws of art *and* nature. But then—

"Hero, wait!" I heard from the back of the P.O. where the sorting happens. Bertie, Mrs. Percy's assistant ran up to the front with a delivery in hand. "Found this in the bottom of the mailbag. Gosh, don't know how long it's been there." They both knew I'd been waiting for a special dispatch, although I hadn't specified what, wanting to keep my project under wraps and the town's mockery to a bearable minimum. Not that either Mrs. Percy or Bertie would indulge, but word gets out.

Bertie handed it to me and we three gazed at it with...??? As Mark Twain once said, "A thing long expected takes the form of the unexpected when at last it comes." Mr. Twain, old pal, you can say *that* again.

Not long ago I'd received an equally perplexing missive from Nile. Another postcard, but unlike his mother's this one depicted a night view of Sudbury's slag heaps, and on the back contained no message whatsoever.

"*Why* didn't he write anything?" Mrs. Percy had asked. Clearly, this was an offense to someone who'd dedicated her life to putting correspondence into people's hands. "Why bother?"

"Yeah, waste of space."

"The strong silent type, is he?"

More the pungent illiterate type. He *did* get my name right, more or less, and while pleased to hear from him, felt somewhat troubled about the molten gushing slag, however scenic, in case this represented some sort of sly commentary on me. (At least he hadn't written, "Wish you were here.")

So I greeted this new oddball communication warily. I didn't recognize the hand, the script wobbly and faint, as if it had received a fright. But then, I don't suppose it's easy to write on birchbark, which is what the envelope was made of. The bark was brownish like the kind used for those overpriced, ersatz birchbark canoes and tipis for sale at Pock's, plump as a French pastry, and, presumably, packed with some sort of communicative filling. I could tell that both Bertie and Mrs. Percy were dying for me to open it, but, in case it was someone's idea of a practical joke, and not requiring a homeo-pathic dose of humiliation at the moment, said airily, "Ahh, finally." Clutching the thing with enough force to make it crack, I then sauntered out of the P.O. as nonchalantly as possible.

Retreating with my 'treasure' to the town docks, I settled on a bench much scored and scarred with lov-ers' initials. Kind of like sitting on a wooden quilt. I couldn't help but notice Douggie's name gouged here and there, often accompanied with primitive and sur-prisingly rude pictographs.

I didn't rip into my own arboreal billet-doux right away, if that's what I had in hand, wanting to sniff it out first. Entirely possible that I had an admirer and I took a moment to consider the candidates: Wes, who sat behind me in Science class (your basic anthropoid); Norm, who worked at the gas station (Spam with teeth and hair); Ned, the minister's son (sex appeal of a lamp); Gord, farmer's progeny (the original green man); Atholl, preening tiddlywinks champion (name sums him up). Would any of these prospective suitors sheath their desires, however tepid, in birchbark? To be sure, none of the Ojibway guys I knew would be caught dead making something as uncool and cornball as this.

Studying the handwriting on the envelope, it occurred to me that my correspondent might be quite young—given the calligraphy, about nine years old.

How long *had* the letter been stuck in the bottom of the mailbag? This thought I found moderately disturbing, for as a recent exile from childhood myself, I was simply too young to be a pedophile. While aware of everyone in town over a certain age, I didn't keep track of all of the younger kids, who tended to travel in an undifferentiated swarm. Unbeknownst to me, some sweet boy might be swooning, heart beating wildly, every time we crossed paths. If I discovered his identity, perhaps I could raise him—you know, like livestock—for enjoyment when mature.

Time to delve deeper.

Fingers spidering as sensitively as a safecracker over the fiercely glued back flap, I managed to jimmy open the envelope without entirely destroying it. After winkling out a thick wodge of lined three-ring paper, I set the envelope aside and immersed myself in a chronicle sent to me from an unidentified 'Camp.' At this point in my life, I did not know that such places existed, nor that children were sent to these woodsy venues in the summer to engage in all manner of ridiculously fun things: hiking, canoeing, swimming, archery, eating s'mores and practising mouth to mouth resuscitation (not necessarily in that order), and making crafts. Evidently, I was in possession of one such *craft*, plus a charmingly uncrafty letter, which, introduced by the simple salutation, "Hi!", went into considerable detail about the above activities, while radiating so much innocence the paper appeared to be lit by some internal source.

The margins of the letter were as richly illustrated as the *Book of Kells,* and while technically challenged (not a great advert for Jon Gnagy if he'd been involved),

I admired their documentary nature nonetheless. Here was something I could relate to: a skunk the size of a moose gassing fellow campers, swimmers fleeing from bloody shark-infested northern waters, and a camp counsellor flat-out with a bottle of poisoned hooch in hand. Uncertain as to whether this was intended as comedy or a cry for help, I decided to settle on the former. The letter drew to a close with, "Luv, Em," and the drawing of a half-eaten hotdog with legs.

A girl-crush, then. Emma? Emily? Some astute, unknown miss who idealized me to the degree that I'd become her imaginary friend? I didn't half-mind the thought of being imaginary. It made me feel light and sort of tingly. As I looked out across the water, letting Lips, a fellow-imaginary being, twiddle delicately with my hair (Lips, wind god, southwest) (note: the wind is *not* called Mariah), I thought about this young girl at Camp Wapawopawipiskwat (just a guess), who might easily have been a younger me (if the parents had ever gotten it together): gut-wrenchingly homesick and lonely, sure, but living on the feral and liberated side of weird.

Deciding to give the letter pride of place in my room, between the snow globe and the dried worm on my dresser, I wedged it back into the envelope, wondering what ingenious object Em might manufacture with my two leftover popsicle sticks, and carried it home, rough and warm in my hand. The feeling of lightness stuck with me, and perhaps for that reason I began to fantasize about that half-eaten hotdog, an annoyingly mobile snack.

No car in the driveway, so either it had been reclaimed, or the folks were at Neath's bar, healing their rift with some liquid first aid. Good, another loan might be in order, especially if the cupboards were bare. I'd have to be quick, though. Guaranteed they'd be back soon—they were like cats, out, in, out, in, never having gotten the hang of what a home is for.

This strategy ran into a snag all too soon on my discovery that I didn't have the place to myself. A woman sat lounging in my father's ratty, hand-me-down La-Z-Boy, gazing into a hand mirror that looked suspiciously like my mother's, while plucking her chin hairs with over-large tweezers, also familiar. This stranger was done up in a style that might best be described as parodic cleaning lady, a smidge too frumpy to be authentic.

"Hello, dear," she said, not looking up.

"Excuse me, who—?"

"Gotcha!" She held up a wiry black hair for assessment before dropping it on the floor. Returning again to the mirror, she angled her chin, thick as an elbow, this way and that, inspecting the cosmetic work site.

I could almost feel my brain moving in my head like a disturbed animal, shifting and resettling, renegotiating its comfy spot. Was she some unknown relative, a member from the dark and distant reaches of the family? You never knew what sort of creature, long-entangled in our genetic coils, might tumble out and land at your feet. (As Auntie Viv says, "The trouble with family, eh, is that they're not the kind of people you'd normally invite into your home.")

"I'm your boarder." Big smile.

Boarder? All the stuff from my room, including my comics and my useless hair dryer in its vinyl zip case *and* my dried worm, had been dumped in a corner of the living room. Here I'd assumed that an unprecedented round of housework had occurred in my absence, but no. *My* room had been rented out? Surely the parents weren't that desperate! (This aggrieved plaint, despite the many bills bookmarking my person.)

Tightening my grip on the birchbark letter, my sole unsullied possession, I gave the encroacher, her with overgrown cuticles, my most searing look, a sort of indignation-radiation combo. (Works for Molly Colossus.)

"You must change your life," she said.

What? Bullshit. But because I had been properly brought up, I didn't say that. I said rather, as Molly herself would say, "That's !@&!#%! bullshit."

"Tsk."

The woman studied me for a tick, then, tossing the mirror and tweezers aside, reached down to the floor and seized a chubby leather purse, black and knobbled as a diseased liver. Settling it on her lap, she unclasped it and began rummaging around inside. I got the impression that she was going to try pacifying me with some laughable token, a candy or a trinket. Or… a gun? Or worse, more unwanted advice. Another gem, say, involving my much maligned oral apparatus, facial feature of the day. (*The closed mouth swallows no flies.*)

And damned if she didn't pluck out of her purse a fortune-cookie-sized slip of paper. After quickly and frowningly perusing it, however, she did not then intone, as you might expect, "Your dearest wish will come true." Nor, "When hungry, order more Chinese food."

Instead, she enquired, "This *is* Ballentine Street, isn't it?"

"*No.*" Ballentine? You *kidding*?

"Hmn." She hauled herself out of the chair and patted herself down, rearranging her brown dress, and, dipping her fingers into a pocket of her equally brown, muskrat-collared jacket, extracted a small silver key. "Here," she said, handing it to me.

As you may imagine, I accepted this key in great surprise and with a surge of wonder. *Was* it? Could it *really* be? Did I finally have in my possession the instrument I needed to give me total access?

And yet… how fragile wonder is. Mine lasted only as long as it took for our unexpected guest to hustle out, heels clacking as she passed my parents on the stairs.

"Who was *that*?" Mother examined the surroundings, puzzled, as though she'd never seen the place before.

"Don't know." Downmarket fairy godmother?

"What did she want?"

"She gave me this." I showed her the key.

"My God." Mother snatched it out of my hand and roared into the folks' bedroom, where she began to make a remarkable amount of racket shoving aside the chest of drawers and yanking up the floorboards.

"Behind every great man stands a large woman," observed Father, proudly.

Molly C might have appreciated the intended compliment, but luckily mother was out of earshot. We, on the other hand, could hear her clearly.

"That *bitch*," she howled. "Robbed! We've been robbed… *ripped off.*" A pause followed this assertion, broken shortly after by some accounting, "She *stole* three dollars. And, and… *five* cents! Five!"

Sounded about right, no further commentary required. After all, hadn't silence been urged upon me all day?

The upshot of this inconvenient trespass? Another move, and this to a hovel about as far away from Ballentine Street as it's possible to get. The starvation-diet reasoning that nourished our exodus? My stuff, positioned closer to the front door than to my room, the parents viewed as a kind of readiness-is-all portent. Plainly, greener pastures beckoned. Even those, as it turned out, splatted with cow pies. As Confusion say, "Home is the thing with legs."

Actually, he didn't say that, *I* did. And can you blame me?

# Juno Pluvia

My cousin? Nile? Never mind, file him under women's troubles and forget about him.

We have other coronary matters to consider. For instance, the unnamed man who washed up on the beach, and who provoked what is called an 'equivocal death analysis.' Of course, it *was* Nile who found him, no getting around that. With his verminous instincts, he managed to upstage the flies, which came tumbling after him in a busy buzzing mass. The lake coughed up the man and served him on a bed of dried marsh grass, an impromptu nest that would have crackled with his sodden weight, a sound that no one heard, no one human. Unless Nile, owl eared, had been listening with his usual predatory acuity.

This surprise stiff was very well preserved for someone who had been dead for five years, a statistic determined by the forensic analysis, I'm not making it up. The cold water had kept him relatively fresh. The guy didn't look that much different than Aunt Faith, who, regrettably, was still alive. He'd been on an epic journey, an underwater Ulysses cruising like a wayward flesh torpedo along the lake bottom, sliding smoothly past schools of fish and over logs, shooting into the broken hull of a sunken schooner. A nightmare man months snagged in the tumbled rigging, then exploding out of a porthole.

He owned a cottage on Lake Michigan, a black Speedo bathing suit, and a gold chain. Early morning, a quick dip, that was the plan. Coffee, a healthy knob of butter glistening on a stack of pancakes (or flapjacks, this being the States), and a Lucky Strike cigarette— irony at its most gauche—smoked down to the filter and flicked into the crapper with a gratifying *hissss.* Simple pleasures for what may or may not have been a complicated man. Crossing a watery border into another country had not been on the day's agenda. Somewhere along his circuitous trip to the morgue (and I have a very good idea where), he lost the gold chain. But not the Speedo. Nothing like a bit of bloat to firmly secure such a slinky scrap of cloth. How many people said, *I wouldn't be caught dead wearing...* before realizing and choking it off with a laugh.

Our mystery man—underwater ambassador (of considerable puffery) and self-made raft borne in on a swift succession of bright waves—eventually acquired a scanty if disappointingly dull covering of detail. Who, how, where. But at first his whole provocatively intact body gleamed with possibility. In his silence, he seemed to insist that we cobble our rural wits together in order to grant him an identity worth all the trouble taken on his incredible journey. Plus the cost of the fare.

Fine, fine. Honour the dead, however unwelcome, sing his praises, if unearned (*anyone* can drown—how hard can it be?), build him a cairn out of a disassembled fire pit. Go crazy. What *I* wanted to know, the sliver of truth to be plucked from this corporal hunk of drift-wood, was the real reason for Nile's opportune presence. By this time, you see, I'm afraid I'd taken an interest. In *him,* Nile, if you can believe it.

"Watch out for that cousin of yours, Hero," Mother warned.

"Why?"

"*Don't* get into his car."

"Why?"

"Don't ask."

Words. Like chipping away with a chisel. I some-times think she returned from her own so-called travels simply to warn me about the exact things she contin-ued to do herself. I was what, fifteen? (Practically, for all intents and purposes.) Nile twenty-five. Do the math. These numbers belonged together—a sequence orderly, beautiful, inevitable (if you can count past ten). Just dig the equation of this perfect pairing: him + me, cousin + cousin, smartass + smarty-pants = 1 hot unit.

Chemistry? We had that, too.

Honestly, I didn't see the problem. Or, I should say, that *was* the problem: Keeping the slimy bastard—and not the one prone on the beach—in sight. He haunted the edge of everything. If you had twenty-twenty vision, he'd go twenty-one, a touch beyond seeing… and believing. My lying quarry, up to no good and not taking the least bit of trouble to deck it out in credible finery, as I might.

So what had he been doing so far from town on this southern shore on this part of the lake not shy about horking up the dead?

"Fishin'."

"You were *not* fishing." Nor, at this point, were we discussing nuclear physics.

"That right?"

"Yeah, that's right."

God, why did I bother. Take a look at him. Grease incarnate. And that suspect smell rolling off him? Did he ever *wash?* Grooming aside, he also had a devil burrowing into his heart like a worm mining an apple. I could practically hear it if I got my ear close enough to his chest.

He looks at me, looks away, laughs.

What, what, *what?*

Not that it mattered, despite how I felt, longing shooting out of my head in spikes. Nile wasn't destined to be my first love, the one true thing that I'll needlessly wreck and never forget, spawning the seductive figure who will slip out of the shadows and into my dreams even when I'm an old bat. No, Nile was emotional mulch, the preparatory ground, romantic tilth. I wanted to sink my hands into this fertile earth deeply, deeply. Eros' apprentice gardener.

My mother needn't have worried, if worry the motivation. Never was I invited into his plush, sex-lit sanctum on wheels. Nile had no compunction whatsoever about feeling up anything remotely female, livestock and minerals included. But, now of age, he would not touch me!

"You're skinny," he said. "You look like a drowned rat." Or, more winningly, "What nose did they pick you out of? Eh, Scuts?"

Ah, fond family talk. I wondered, though, didn't he know the difference between a cousin and a sister?

Yes, yes, all right, while my future physique might best be described as Junoesque, I was presently more goddess-nascent. Larval, if you will. I knew I had potential, because I'd begun to catch looks from boys my own age. Guys without cars, muscles, chest hair, wallets with chains, swagger, dirty yellow combs sticking out of their back pockets, and smokes glued to their bottom lips. I kept an eye on their manly development nonetheless. Juno Fidia.

His girlfriends? No contest, all cross-eyed and bucktoothed, I kid you not. Some were fat, some halt, and some so old they obviously needed elastic bands on their underwear to hold them together and keep them upright. Body bags, all. Generously, Nile paid them court, indiscriminately portioning out his charms. A single focus, one girlfriend only, even one bejewelled with a goiter, would have been a more dangerous proposition, unless the one girlfriend happened to be me. Not that I can't be dangerous, especially when riled. Juno Fulminator.

Nile in love? A disturbing thought.

I flipped through the phone book to see who might be living in the island's southern reaches, in some enchanted cedar scrub populated by the inbred, the unemployed, and perhaps a witch. Or a siren, working the beach, who may have called out to a corpse bobbing irresolutely in the water and convinced it to call it a day, to come sculling in like a lonely seal and lie at her feet. RIP, my pet.

Mother snapped her fingers in my face, told me to stop mooning around, do the dishes, do *something*. I shifted to my room, slammed the door, and hurled myself onto the bed, at one with my discarded clothes, a host of selves slaughtered by ill-use. My childhood hovered beguilingly close. There'd be no retreating, though, no more whirling carefree down the road on my bike, no more spinning dizzily on the tire swing out back, pulling my immediate world down a drain hole vortex. Undeniably I was sick, infected with maturity.

But this thing, please don't call it puppy love. It was more like something that ate puppies.

Fact is, I was older than Nile in many ways. My command of language, for one. Always silver tongued, I could now spin gold, forging one aureate link after another. Listening to me (I think he listened), the best Nile could do was swill beer, nod, belch.

Evidently, there would be no catching him in a linguistic snare. My campaign required actions, not words. Mother commanded me to do something? Okay then, I will, I most definitely will.

My friend Beatrice, usually firm in her sympathies, regarded me with alarm. Her naturally bulgy eyes bulged a degree more.

"You're not serious, are you?"

"Darn tootin'."

"Hero?"

"What?"

"This is not a good idea, you know that."

"Why don't you come, too?"

"Hah. Parents."

Bea's parents were less distracted than mine, a feature of our domestic arrangement that I'd be counting on. Her parents rarely left the house, their own bulgy eyes relentless in surveillance.

"Sluts," she shook her head in wonder. "Tramps."

Bea's own verbal reach was modest, but she managed to produce the essentials as required. In this instance referring to the kind of women who attended the Saturday night dances held in the boathouse on the town dock, dances that not infrequently featured vile language, vile manners, punch-ups, knives, random grunting, and adulterous scrabbling in dark corners. In other words über-adult affairs. If Nile was to be found anywhere, this was the place.

"I'm going."

"You've got to wear a skirt."

"A *skirt?* Jesus!"

"And a bra."

"_____!"

Getting out of the house on the night of my romantic crusade was a snap. All week, I half-expected my parents to deviate from their usual behaviour and unwittingly throw a spanner into the works, some plot complication in our ongoing family sitcom to bugger things up. On Saturday, perchance alerted by my unsolicited bout of hygienic activity (washed hair, brushed teeth), I feared they would smell a rat (one with a dab of Evening in Paris behind each ear) and, in an unprecedented move, award me with the full blessing of their attentions. Make popcorn, break out the Monopoly board, attempt conversation, or dumb jokes, and basically seal up the windows and doors with a gluey clan ambience.

But no, Mother's fork had barely cooled on the dinner table before she'd peeled away down the drive, off to bingo. ("Hell, I'd shout 'Bingo,' too, if he was that good," says Auntie Viv.) Father ambled into the living room, flicked on the TV, flomped onto the worse-for-wear La-Z-Boy, kicked off his shoes, wiggled his toes, yawned, scratched his chin. Gone.

So no complications. I didn't even bother to slide pillows under the bedcovers and sculpt them into a sur-rogate self. Who would look in later to check on me to see if I was all right—in situ angelic and unharmed, or out boogying the night away? Children's Aid? The actual sitcom remained confined to the tube, unspool-ing viewer-free as I snuck out, while our particular plot remained predictable, if unfathomable.

Once out of doors, the question of transportation arose. Options: take the bike to town, or be transported along the shore on my own sneaker-shod feet. The road would be quicker but came with perils, mainly from a Saturday night spike in traffic. A pastoral spike, inter-mittent at best, but still. I risked recognition, dust up my nose, and agonizing death in the ditch at the heedless hands of a driver half-cut and with his tongue planted not in his cheek, but in his lady friend's waxy ear. This thought was so revolting that I decided on the shore.

No need to hurry. Things didn't heat up at the dance until dark, and with the boathouse crowded and lights dimmed for body contact activities, I planned to slip in unnoticed. I could afford the dawdling more than I could the cover charge. Or being turfed out before Nile had a chance to take me under his wing, fledgling vamp that I was.

I passed some time on the shore, skipped some stones, sat on my favourite rock, roosting on fossils, haz-arding hemorrhoids. With night well on its way—Nyx in flowing, funereal dress advancing across the sky, black chariot, black horses—cold began to seep into the rock, chilling my little cheeks. Trouble with skirts, they let in too much of the outside world.

"Picture yourself twirling," Beatrice had urged, her saleswoman future already in force as she thumbed through the borrowable stock in her closet.

Friends, it wasn't me. A plaid, pleated number, browny orange, that fell below my knees. What finally clinched it? The thing was reversible, a feature I'm a sucker for, whether in a product or a human (figuratively speaking). The reverse side wasn't all that different, a browny green plaid, but I liked the idea of a secret skirt and making a quick switch in mid-manic-twirl, *hey presto*, part dervish, part magician. Wouldn't that just floor them.

Halfway to town, much darker now, waves chatting up the shoreline, I began to wonder what it might be like to stumble across a floater. In island life, always a possibility. Like the man from Michigan, deceased water-borne tourists did occasionally show up requiring accommodation. With visibility low to nil, a person might easily trip over one and land smack on top of it, sending a fountain of lake water leaping out of its mouth.

Nile hadn't seemed troubled in the least about his beach find, but then his life's mission was to cause trouble, not feel its effects.

I picked up the pace. (I ran.)

The place was hopping when I got there, live band, The Blacksmiths, they were terrible. I hung around on the dock, crouched behind a pile of junk—coiled ropes, nets, wooden crates, a broken outboard—and caught a lucky break when the guy manning the ticket booth went out for a piss and a smoke. Slipping in, I navigated the wall, finding the most shadowy spot from which to observe the goings-on. I'm telling you, it was a study. Fast dances, slow dances. During the slow ones, couples tried to crawl inside each other, and during the fast ones they couldn't get far enough apart, bobbing their heads, shaking their fat deposits, writhing like they were covered in snakes and trying to fling them off.

I knew most everyone there except the out-of-towners, and I'll admit to being shocked when I discovered Miss Lewis, the grade five teacher, among them. In my drippy skirt, *I* looked more like a schoolteacher than she did with her high heels, tight pants, tight top, and scarlet lips. (Wait till Bea hears about *this*.) Strutting past, Douggie Williams was so busy leering at her that he failed to notice a puddle of puke dead on, stepped in it, then sailed across the room executing an ace triple lutz before felling Hercules Orr, pinboy at the bowling alley who, while no stranger to missiles heading his way, was too impressed to leap aside. The room burst into wildly appreciative hoots and guffaws.

Have to admit, I was enjoying myself. I settled back, sticking to the wall like adhesive, when out of the steamy miasma, composed of sweat, bad breath, booze, and eau de earthworm (the boathouse sold bait during the day), a skeletal hand reached out, latched onto mine, and yanked me into the fray. Some guy, a total stranger, scraggy and old, needing dental work and hair.

"Hey, baby," he said, looking me up and down, grinning. "Left yer tits at home, didja?"

I took this to be a rhetorical question, and frankly I was too stunned by the appearance of this spectre to respond.

"Take off, dipshit."

Not me saying it (though it should have been), for Hero's hero—undetected up till now—had arrived! Nile applied his palm to the side of the guy's head and shoved. *Crick* went the interloper's neck.

"*Watch it, asshole. I found 'er first.*"

"Fuck off," Nile said, so casually I gave him a thumbs-up. Such class.

And seeing as he came with a complete set of toned biceps, currently on display, my geriatric date did as advised, spitting expletives as he stumbled through the crowd.

Nile stared at me.

"What are you doing here?"

"It's a dance, yeah? I *can* dance, you should see me. Want to? Let's, c'mon. It's really something, you know. How I can dance. . . ."

"Listen." He slid his dangerous hands into his pockets, looked down at his pointy shoes, looked up at me. Dark eyes intent. He sighed, softly. But, magic in the air, that sigh had enough wind power to scatter the prohibition that had been placed upon me like a spell. He reached out, both hands, touched my hair and hooked it behind my ears. He trailed his fingers down my neck, over my shoulders, tenderly smoothing the wrinkles out of my shirt, briefly lingering on the straps of my training bra beneath. He ran his hands slowly down my arms and gently held me by my wrists.

"Go home."

Exactly what you might say to a dog.

"How? Will you drive me?"

"Can't."

"Why not?"

"Don't ask."

He relinquished his hold and turned away. My own hands fell limp at my sides as I watched him move like liquid past the band and out of the open doorway. About to follow—I had no intention of letting him escape so easily—someone else stepped in front of me, blocking my exit.

"Uh, want to dance?"

Matt Finch. A boy from high school, upper grades, tall, not bad looking, but I'm afraid the name Matt suited him to a T; psychologically speaking, he was a clump of tightly wound and interwoven neuroses. Also, since I had a decent view of his shirt, I saw that he had a piece of meat stuck on it. Hot dog fallout, I surmised. A meager sample, but effective in clearing the room. Of me, at least.

"Sorry," I said, dodging around him. "Gotta find my cousin. It's urgent."

"Oh, don't," I heard him say to my retreating back. "Don't go out."

Have I ever been accused of listening to sound advice? I have not. I went out.

Not a soul on the dock, strangely. No couples out for a breather, a smooch, a dance that might advance into the lake, depending on their level of blood alcohol.

And no Nile. Typical. The more I wanted to see him, the less I saw. My man, making himself scarce, rationing himself out. The secret of his success (and my failure).

I raced down the length of the dock to the parking lot. A tactical error. His car sat motionless in the dust, as forsaken as me. The band, venue-sensitive if nothing else, was playing "Smoke on the Water," loudly, but not so loud that it masked the sound of an outboard starting up. A Peterborough, by the sounds of it. I loved being out in a powerboat at night, tearing along, pure freedom—or a convincing enough illusion of it.

I loved it a whole lot more than sitting on the splintery end of the dock, digging my nails into my knees and sucking in motor oil fumes as I watched the water cresting in the boat's wake. So it wasn't *my* hair that the wind reverently tousled. Nor was that luminous, ghost-white dress, fluttering so evocatively, worn by me. I knew her—all too well—but my brain refused the information, keeping her safely generic, blank as her dress. (What would our family do without the faculty of denial?)

I wondered if they stole the boat. Both stood in the bow, not touching, she steering, facing the open water.

Where Nile had touched me it hurt, as if he'd laid down a trail of bruises or burns on my skin.

I raised my hand to my chest, too late to protect myself, and felt something lumpy in my shirt pocket. Digging in, I pulled out a gold chain. *The* gold chain, grave robber's loot, and a gift as dexterously given as it was perplexing. If our Michigan friend, pre-autopsy, remained a mystery, he wasn't a patch on Nile. Cut *him* open and you'd be no wiser.

Pouring the chain from hand to hand, this hand, that hand, my heart contracted, pitiful and pitiless. I imagined a dark shape moving in the water below, and with a self-conferred power of occult redress payed the chain into the lake, righting all indignities. I looked up at the starless night sky and imagined rain, a hard, painful, obliterating downpour.

And then it came.

# Closer

Let me tell you something. I have resources, not your typical. I'm a bona fide conduit of strange. And something else. Think darkest, what I'm after, what I can almost reach. It's like a treasure resting on the bottom of the lake, a lost lure festooned with hooks. A cruel thing. I keep trying and trying.

In the meantime, I'm sixteen. I am not sweet. I'm steeped in ignorance and yet I know everything, as any respectable sixteen year old should. Not only the goings-on in town—the affairs, the swindles, the vendettas—and the family secrets—dirty or slight or searing—but the more arcane goods, harder to come by. I have no need to make withdrawals from the community loose-lips fund.

Also, I have these new power tools, hormonally acquired, it's amazing what they can do. But I'm in no rush to use them. The current boyfriend is smitten. (Note: Am using the term 'current' loosely here as 'first' might give the wrong impression.) He's head over heels, although you'd never know it from some of the things he says. Of my most recent school photo, proudly presented, he observes, "You look like a witch."

Well well well. Look who's dishing out a simile. Unwittingly. *You are a witch*, might have been closer to the mark. But the mark he usually misses. As he fumblingly slides the photo into a plastic sleeve of his tan cowboy-boot embossed wallet, I give him the once-over. Acne minimal, flop of reddish golden hair adorning his brow, standard issue nose, good teeth—visible, on account of his mouth hanging open. (Okay, lips slightly parted.) (Soft lips, mm-hmm). All in all not an embarrassment. Thus he earns a reprieve, although he needs beware. I know a curse that deployed will suck his head through the neck hole of his freshly laundered Fruit-of-the-Loom T-shirt, lickety-split and without a single feature left lagging.

"X," he says.

I'm not listening.

"XXX," he says, louder, more insistently.

Don't press your luck, chum.

I have more on my mind than boys boys boys. For example, because I know everything and my high school teachers obviously don't, I've decided to extend to them my sympathetic interest and, more importantly, my assistance. This benighted group is so locked in the students' comedic conception of them that they're scarcely real. Cutouts, two-dimensional, jokers and cartoons. They're oddballs I'll grant you that, but, rolling up my sleeves and cracking the knuckles on my capable and lovely hands, I am prepared to grant them a dimension.

With the exception of Miss Cosima, who is a bit too real for my liking and an object (note: object) of those very boys boys boys' fascination and depraved speculation. This despite her advanced years. More troubling, I understand that she's been seen hanging around with my cousin Nile. Dangerous company to keep, wouldn't wish that on anyone, so some disenchantment definitely required there.

Nile himself has always been a trickier proposition. He knows to keep well beyond my range, coming and going, now in town, now not. I might catch sight of him peeling out of the Tasty Freeze 'Home of the Footlong Hotdog' parking lot, flicking a butt through the vent window, or with his arm slung around some gal, her bale of teased dirty blonde hair skewed sideways. He works off-island, for a time in the mines, lately at the Bruce nuclear power plant, which might explain his toxic glow. You never know when he'll show up, dropping in on his folks for a brew and a fight. They all love it, this explosive touchdown. Twenty minutes in, visit over, he saunters away up the front walk, leaving my Uncle Earl cradling his busted fist in his armpit and Aunt Faith panning for gold as she filters a dross of threats through a screen door that's been slammed with percussive finesse.

My own home life is less theatrical, the hurts less entertaining. Which makes it a good place to practise my hocus-pocus philanthropy before going public. Plus I'm still working out the bugs.

"Huh!" says my father, anchored by a sudden silver mine of change in his pockets, a tumorous bulge of wealth appearing on both thighs, pants straining to plunge to the floor. "Washers?" he says, mystified, pulling a fistful out. "What the—?"

"Morland?" my mother says, quietly, shocked, staring at her reflection in the hallway mirror. "I used to be beautiful, didn't I? What in God's name happened? I look like a *fish*."

On the upside, not such a deplorable metamorphosis, fishermen here being in ready supply. Her band of admirers can only grow.

Besides, none of the above happened. I'm stuck in this reality like everyone else, although I'm convinced I can tweak it, mind over matter (hide your spoons!), regardless of how stubborn or flaccid that matter might be.

Onward then with my sympathy project. But where to begin? With Mrs. Smuts, who teaches Science and is crawling with microbes from never observing the five second rule when she falls down? Which is often. Or the history teacher, Mr. Bruno? The man has a fascinating moss-green patch in his furry hair, slightly pointy ears, and speaks a mongrel English no one understands. Or our French teacher, Mr. O'Hanrahan, who at some point in is life appears to have been taxidermied, odd parts crudely stitched together, which might not be as far-fetched as it sounds because he drives without a license, madly. Should we ever find ourselves in Ireland and requiring a few words of French, our education won't have been in vain. Not only that but I've learned a thing or two in O'Hanrahan's class. "A shroud on you!" he once barked, jovially enough, hexing a farmer kid genetically incapable of conjugating of the verb *être*. I admire this curse, while am not quite sure how it works. The kid subsequently attended a Hallowe'en dance dressed in an unravelling mummy costume over which he tripped, fell, landed on a broken 40-ouncer and sliced open his forehead. Blood everywhere, interesting.

O'Hanrahan being a somewhat dicey proposition, I decide to give him a miss and begin with an easy one, our English teacher, Mrs. Dumpty. Seriously, Dumpty. There are places one doesn't venture with a name like that and a school is one of them. So trust me, I didn't invent it, although I have no doubt that the 'Mrs.' honorific is a fiction of her own making and that—plastic bag, twist tie—she's been stored on the matrimonial shelf since the day she emerged from virginal girlhood. If Miss Cosima is a vision that dazzles the boys, then Mrs. Dumpty, to put it kindly, is not. They can hardly muster enough derision to concoct more than a lame dribble of "Humping Dumpty" cracks, presumably because the idea is too grotesque. For her own part, she wears a permanent expression of dismay at finding herself marooned in a corner of the country where civilization has not reached. On her first day in class she had tried, gamely, to plumb the depths by surveying our literary knowledge:

"*The Mayor of Casterbridge?*"

Blank stare. Bovine chewing.

"*A Tale of Two Cities?*"

An overloud gas leak.

"*Wuthering Heights?* Anyone?"

My hand shot up. I hadn't actually read it, of course, but was aware of its existence, seeing as my Auntie Viv used a copy of this very book at her place to prop up the game leg of a wobbly end table. I only meant to give the woman a restorative dose of encouragement, but by displaying a spark of intellectual accomplishment had unintentionally endeared myself to her. From here on in she paid me particular attention, as though I were some sort of float that might save her from drowning. She brought in books she thought I might like, which she handed to me in secret after class so as not to expose me to ridicule. (Not bloody *likely*.) I lugged some home, stored most of them in my locker, and flatly refused others, like one called *The Feminine Mystique*. I had absolutely no desire to learn about makeup and feminine wiles. Wiles I am sufficiently endowed with, and believe you me, they are beyond feminine.

This made her smile, something we rarely saw, and she said, "Maybe later, Hero, when you're a little older."

Sure, sure. Thing was I needed to do some research on my chosen subject and concocted a plan that, ignoble even from my point of view, worked. Last class of the day, perfect. I knew where she'd be, while she would have no idea where I was headed.

"Cramps," I moan, discreetly indicating my nether region.

"Off you go then, dear," she says. "No need to sign out."

Hippity-hop I hasten downtown to her apartment, which is on the top floor of The Bakers' Daughter's Bakery (no time to explain, though can't fault the punctuation—someone knows what they're doing—other than me). Fortunately, access to the apartment is up an enclosed set of back stairs, so I scoot up unseen, lift the doormat for the key, which is where *everyone* hides theirs, and find zip. Damn! I examine the windows, which are sealed tight, then try the door anyway, glad-handing the knob like an upbeat mortician… and it opens. What a trusting soul, I think, which causes a ghostly wisp of guilt to flit through me as I enter. The place is tidy and homey, if depressingly furnished with second-hand stuff—small sitting room, kitchen, bedroom—and smells distractingly of doughnuts, the Bakers' daughter, Doris Baker's specialty.

I don't waste any time snooping, although the bedroom is a temptation, but head straight for the bathroom and the medicine chest. They don't call it a chest for nothing. Secrets close to the heart are stored there, evidence of griefs and pains, aspirations and failings, compulsions and desires. All I need to know I will find behind the mirrored door of this cabinet (into which I gaze fleetingly before opening—I look pretty damn good, eyes, hair, I'm impressed). So I open it up and *cripes* the very first thing I discover, the very *first* leaves me reeling. Reeling! Confusion momentarily reigns.

Cautiously, I lift it out, a round plastic case, clear on the front with a turquoise backing, which contains within a circular arrangement of yellow pills. Birth control pills. My friend Beatrice and I had discovered one like this buried deep in her mother's underwear drawer. At least Bea's mother had the decency to hide it, rather than leaving it practically out in the open where someone young and impressionable might find it. What on earth is Mrs. Dumpty doing with this, though? She can't possibly have any use for these things. Perhaps there *is* a Mr. Dumpty after all. So where is he then? There'd been no sightings as far as I know. Always possible that the pills had been prescribed for another condition altogether, like unhappiness.

I check the prescription label on the front of the dispenser and am immediately relieved to see someone else's name on it: Catherine Dunphy. Don't know her. Nor is there any sign of a roommate. Wait, crap! Dumpty's not her name! But everyone calls her that, likewise the principal, Mr. Bumbershoot. (I know, I *know*. Where does the School Board find these Dickensian rejects? And *yes*, Dickens, I have read some of Mrs. D's proffered books.) *Geez.*

Which is when I get to thinking... I wonder if she'd miss any? Her eyesight's not great, she blinks a lot during class. I might be able to use a smidgen of assistance in the gynecological department myself. There'd been pressure lately from the boyfriend, a petting upgrade appeared to be required, and he'd dropped numerous none too subtle hints about other girls who would be more "considerate." A disgraceful state of affairs. I'm already beginning to miss the days when going all the way meant nothing more compromising than a shopping trip to Woolworth's in Sudbury.

I study the package, which in itself looks impregnable. Substituting another kind of pill doesn't appear to be feasible. (Baby Aspirin would be charmingly ironic, if I had any on hand.) I'm thinking there's good chance that in the morning, half-asleep and running late for school, or drugged on doughnut fumes, she downs her daily pill in a hurry without noticing how many are already gone. Three pills would get me through the weekend, I figure, enough time to give the dirty a whirl and prove that I'm no prude.

I'm not entirely sold on this plan. Isn't there more power in holding out than in caving? Nor do I want to set a man-pleasing precedent. Slippery slope, that. And what if she *does* miss the pills? What would she make of it? Seeing as I'm being scrupulous about leaving no trace of my presence, my best guess is that she'd suspect Doris Baker of sneaking upstairs and pilfering a serving of this bun-in-oven prophylactic. (Ha ha.)

Undecided, but hating to miss an opportunity, I crank out a trio of pills into my palm, then slip them into my shirt pocket. I close the cabinet door, snatch up a face cloth, wipe the frame of fingerprints, and neatly replace the cloth. After quietly exiting the scene of the crime, I go around to the Bakery and buy a doughnut. Chocolate-covered, bliss.

Heading down the walk for home, munching contentedly, Matt Finch slides by me on his bike.

"Hi," he says.

"Hi," I say.

I'm chagrined at this chance encounter because my upper lip now sports a Hitlerian dab of chocolate. Matt has a long-standing crush on me which I fear is nearing its expiry date given the perfunctory nature of his greeting. While always in the one syllable range, his conversation is usually charged with longing. The ill-positioned smear of chocolate may have snuffed it out entirely. Matt is in Grade Thirteen, several grades ahead of me and, lately, inexplicably, has acquired an air of cool that he's never exhibited before. Taking a quick look over my shoulder, I see him turn into the lane that leads to Mrs. D's apartment. Odd.

By the time I've turned round to investigate, he's stashed his bike in a screen of bushes and is eagerly climbing the stairs. Mrs. D might arrive any minute now, I can't imagine what he's up to… and then I get it. Of course! The Departmental Exams, she must be tutoring him. No wonder he sounded curt. The exams are taxing, and one's whole future depends on them. (Note: Not that I'll have a problem when my time comes.) Buoyed by this thought, I nip into the bushes and remove the bicycle clip left dangling from his handlebars. I push up my sleeve, clamp it on my right bicep like a warrior princess, and strike out for home.

Next morning, Friday, I take one of the pills in preparation for the school dance on Saturday night. Down the hatch with the Captain Crunch. Most of the morning I feel fabulously mature and witchy, but by lunch less so. During Phys Ed, first class in the afternoon, after a round of jumping jacks, sit-ups, and a range of other exercises that are later deemed to be hazardous to physical heath, I feel wobbly and weird. Before I keel over, the instructor, Miss Cosima, comes to my rescue.

"Are you all right, Hero?"

Good question at the best of times, but I appreciate her solicitation.

"You look awfully pale," she says, leading me to a chair in a corner while managing to look awfully sexy herself. In sweatpants. (I suspect her of downing *The Feminine Mystique* in one lip-smacking gulp.)

Since I unexpectedly have her ear, I decide to fill it with a poisonous solution.

"Thanks so much, Miss Cosima. It's… I've been worried sick. My older cousin, Nile, you wouldn't know him, it's… shocking."

"Why, what's happened?"

"He—" Think, *think*. "He's run off to South America to join a revolutionary gorilla group." (Get off, I *know* it's guerilla.)

"Oh, *really*," she drawls in that sultry voice of hers, placing a hand on one of her significant hips, painted nails gleaming. "What a bad boy."

Blew it. Rats! I should have told her that Nile had joined the United Church ministry instead.

As I enter English class, Mrs. D gives me a funny look, although offers no solicitations of her own. I don't think much of it, for by this time everyone seems to be giving me funny looks, which I put down to Pill-induced, reality-warping paranoia. Unless the pill I took was some other life-altering chemical, LSD or arsenic, secreted in a birth control package. I'm beginning to clue in to the mystery of Mrs. D's missing spouse and give her my own probing look before wafting out of class.

My brief fling with contraception over, I flush the other two pills down the toilet when I get home. And forget the dance, despite me having given the boyfriend some dangerous ideas as to how the evening will end. By Saturday, I'm restored to rude health, but tell him that I have the flu. Moreover, repossessed of my usual discernment, am all too aware that failing the Departmentals isn't the only thing that can ruin a girl's life. So I stay home, make fudge, and watch Red Skelton reruns with my father. Sitting side by side on the couch and scarfing down the fudge, we both laugh heartily at Red's Heathcliff-and-Gertrude seagull skit. By now I've settled into *Wuthering Heights* and find that this allusion adds a layer of textual richness to the reading experience. Possibly the sugar high helps.

First thing Sunday morning my sanguine mood is blasted to bits by a call from Bea with news about the dance. More specifically, news that the boyfriend left halfway through with Deb Hooker. (These *names*. It's like a morality play. Who's going to show up next? Death?) Bea herself overheard Deb entice the boyfriend by offering to show him her brassiere if he could guess its colour. We all know that! And it's only black because she never washes it. Yet off the horndog goes to dip his wick in the common market. Not only that, but by Monday morning it's clear that I've been dumped before I can extricate myself from the relationship with dignity. Deb smiles and smiles like a villain, but I'm capable of worse, much worse.

In order to augment my bag of tricks, I feel that there's no sense in avoiding Mr. O'Hanrahan any longer and drop by his office under the pretense of researching a history project on Irish folkloric sayings. He's flattered by my interest and soon we get into an exchange of information, a spirited cursing match, like a pair of duelling druids.

"Smothering and drowning on you," he says cheerfully.

"Go soak your head," I counter, getting warmed up.

"Scorching and burning on you."

"Die miserable blundering barbecued blister."

"Captain Haddock?"

"Yep. With a slight amendment."

"Nice. May the devil choke you."

"'Devil take your fingers.'" The Bard, no slouch.

"'Hag-seed hence.'"

Guy knows his Shakespeare. Trying to catch him off-guard, I throw in, "Dirtball!"

*Pog ma thoin!*

"Meaning?"

"Kiss my arse."

Ah, I see. "QI'yaH tabernak!"

"Which is?"

"French Canadian Klingon. Untranslatable."

"Tsk. Lord help us." He thinks, continues with, "May the cat eat you and the devil eat the cat!"

"May your mother stir fry your guts in a wok and serve them on soda bread!" Am *cooking* now. "May the road rise to meet you... and knock out your teeth!"

"*Cac* on ye!"

"Oh *yeah*? Go shit yourself, you bog-trotting frog-eating bug-fucking fairy!!"

Mr. O'Hanrahan looks unexpectedly startled. He blinks at me and his lips part, but *nada*... not a word.

I win! First prize, however, is a detention.

This gives me time to reflect in any event. No one else is in the detention room except me, an errant fly in danger of bashing its brains out on the window, and Mrs. Smuts, face down and sound asleep on the front desk. Watching the fly struggle with an incomprehensible barrier, I'm led to contemplate the limitations of language. It had been a riot hurling curses around like I did there with O'Hanrahan, but seriously who am I trying to fool here? Myself apparently. Subject, verb, object... nothing's lurking in a sentence, really. Nothing dark and twisty. Sticks and stones and all that. Damage is definitely possible with a well-wielded phrase, but you have to be satisfied with subtlety and a scarcely visible emotional bruising. If, say, I wanted to break a few bones—speaking theoretically—I'd have to get my hands on some instruments of a blunter and cruder make than what my tongue alone can forge.

It's a sobering thought, but as the days pass I continue to fiddle with my linguistic weaponry anyway, polishing and tinkering. It gives me a charge and allows me to feel more useful. Although helping the teachers realize some humanity is a misbegotten plan and too tough to accomplish, so I give up on that. Besides, when the very last bell sounds at the end of term, every single one of them will drop everything on the spot in a clatter of books and chalk and empty vodka bottles and flee. You won't be able to see them for dust. And when the dust finally settles there'll be a whole new crop of wackos and weirdos flat as a deck of cards in their place.

Funny thing, though, before the end of term it's Mrs. D. who leaves abruptly. I wouldn't have taken her for a quitter and students were beginning to warm to her, going so far as to crack open a book every once in a while to please her. This was especially hard on Matt Finch, her leaving before the Departmentals. He had to be hospitalized. Nervous prostration. I figure his brain got overheated from all that studying, it happens (though rarely in our town). Plus, his crush on me has grown so severe that it's affected his vocal chords. Guy can't get a single word out when I'm around.

Prom night. The reasons I don't attend are legion. First off, no one asks me. Secondly, the X-boyfriend is taking Deb and I don't relish getting her gloating

Hooker smile snagged in my eye. Thirdly, Miss Cosima is one of the chaperones and will be so resplendent in her sparkly clingy minidress, a less virtuous Diana of the Hunt, that she will outshine every other female there. Fourthly, I'm suffering the effects of a bad perm and my ego would not be bolstered by electrified poodle jests at this point in time. Fifthly—have I assembled a legion yet?—I now prefer books to humans. There are worse dates to have for the prom than *Madame Bovary,* believe me. Humans, sadly non-fictional, get drunk and act like idiots and drive headlong into the biggest trees they can find. Their endings are rarely happy, but at least with Madame B. you can close the book before things get too out of hand.

So, for old time's sake, I fling a clutch of curses high into the starry night, letting the consequences fall where they may, and hold my peace.

Next day, I happen to notice a fly-sized speck on the horizon that appears to be rapidly growing in visibility. Nile, I soon discover, zeroing in on me, not his usual mode of entry into my orbit. I don't like the looks of this and would cut and run if there were any chance of escape. He doesn't stop, only gets closer and closer until I smell a wave of grass (both kinds) and sweat and he's standing in front of me, desirable despite the pungency, but only if he doesn't speak. The hair on my arms rises with a soft *whoosh*.

He says, "Last night. Accident."

No waste of words, but I get the message.

"You're kidding, right? Nile? Tell me you're kidding."

"I am," he says, "not."

"Miss Cosima?" I wince.

He shakes his head, then bends closer, his lips grazing my ear, about to fill it with the names of the dead, but all he whispers is, "Hero, what have you done?"

# More Rats Later

One day, when I was old enough to have a job, but not old enough to drink, or to vote, or do anything even remotely interesting, I lost my parents. They did not die, a feat that would have been more straightforward and comprehensible. No, no, not their way. Rather, they, and all their worldly goods, vanished. This stagey piece of business occurred between the time I left for work in the morning and the time I returned home for lunch. The last I saw of them they'd been seated at the breakfast table, listless and dishevelled, picking the sleep out of their eyes and staring dazed into their coffee cups, apparently defeated by the effort required to lift them to their lips. As far as I could tell they had no plans for the day, nor for the many to follow.

We were living in town then, a short walk from my summer job at Scully's to the house we were renting. *They* were renting with their quickly diminishing funds. I contributed zilch to the kitty, not a lick practical or existential, except my youthful good looks and irritatingly precocious wit. Be that as it may, I saw this as no reason to leave me in the lurch, orphaned and homeless, while yet in full expectation of a fried bologna sandwich and glass of milk. *Years* of sustenance, if not joy, being far less delusional than my forebears.

Running up the front steps and onto the porch, I found the front door locked. The flimsy curtain that usually graced the door's window was missing, so I peered in, while rattling the knob and giving the door a good hard kick. Shading my eyes against the sun's glare, I saw clearly what I couldn't see. The place had been cleaned out. Furniture, rugs, pictures, dishes, knickknacks, orange peels and bottle caps in disordered display on the floor… gone. Every material thing that makes a home workable, never mind how hideous or insignificant, was gone. The other two material things that generally made my life miserable were also gone. The shits!

No explanatory note taped to the window. No hint, no clue. Not a suspect smear of DNA on the doorframe, nor a telltale clot of blood sucked into the doormat. No doormat.

I retreated to the front stoop and sat down, facing the road, turned against the view at my back. The house rested on a hill that overlooked the downtown, the town docks—at that time lined with yachts and sailboats—the channel, the bridge, and the mountains in the distance beyond. I didn't think that scanning the terrain below me for evidence of the parents' whereabouts would help. Their escape had been too accomplished, too sealed and complete for them to be swaggering around below, newly unburdened, having cast off parenthood along with domesticity's ills and bills.

*Jezuss,* though. Regardless of how slick the operation, they'd run away from home like two rascally kids. Not that a merry jape of this sort was unprecedented in town. A year ago a whole family, the Plotts—parents, nippers, hamster—had run away. They took off in the husband's girlfriend's car, and boy, was she steamed. So not an original stunt by any means.

All the same, I couldn't figure out how they'd pulled it off. Or *why.* Wasn't I the nucleus of this nuclear family? Moving takes time. I'd witnessed enough of it to know. Innumerable boxes to fill, and for that reason, innumerable smokes, naps, and arguments to bolster resolve. Or at least to get the job over with. The folks had come unstuck of late—this house, that house, as if the right combination of lumber, shingles, and Insulbrick might comfortably house all dissatisfactions. I'd learned to keep my eye on the road.

The stretch of road that lay before me I knew well, although our tenancy in the house had been relatively brief. (*I'll say.*) Not that I had the pebbles all tallied, but I was fondly familiar with its ambitious potholes, its bald patches, its silky fine dust that ghosted my shoes. At midday and at dusk I followed it home, an ever reliable ascent, and in evening we descended together into the shadowy parts of town where, not to reveal anything too discreditable, some groping admittedly occurred with a fellow-mortal of my acquaintance.

So… the road to freedom? I could easily follow this homely byway down the hill, join its smoother paved brother at the bottom, and hot-foot it out of town. I could bugger-off like the parents and not be to blame. Assuming that anyone should happen to notice. *Most* parents who lose their offspring suffer terribly all their livelong days. They're *sorry* for it and ache all over and break out in rashes. Somehow I did not feel that this fund of anguish would necessarily accrue in my case. Might be better to stick around. Besides, I suspected that the road before me—a route blessed with a canine's loyalty and a design more simple than treacherous—would only lead me back to work.

Rising from the stoop, I turned and took one last look at the house. You can never go home again? Too effing true, it seemed. I felt a keen stab of pity. For myself. A weighty sob circulated in my system like a clunky old-fashioned submersible threatening to surface. (Some *food* might have kept my emotions in check. Glucose has its place.) While in this pre-lachrymose and psychologically vulnerable state, my eye snagged on something indefinable: a shadowy something that slipped away under the porch, too fast for me to identify. If I'm not mistaken (hardly possible), it sported a long barbed tail, cerise-red eyes, fur of a charred-black hue… and horns.

This sighting cast a troubling and somewhat garish light, not upon my ever robust mental health, but upon the mysterious disappearance of my parents. Had they been whisked away by some evil undertow? They and all their stuff, including the bottle caps and orange peels? Was I next? While old enough to be embarrassed by this notion, I was yet young enough to entertain it, and it spooked me. Dithering no longer, I skittered off down the hill.

As predicted, Pavlov's road led me back to work.

Between customers and stints on cash, my friend
Bea and I whiled away the afternoon by playing the
dismembered anatomy game. This involved being dealt
a hand, literally on occasion, consisting of a random
selection of broken mannikin body parts from those
heaped in a corner of the storeroom and artfully placing them in the most cunning spots in the store. Your
guileless shopper might thereby discover a crooked finger poking invitingly out of the modest décolletage of a
housedress, a tearless eyeball nestled in the hankies and
ready to roll if disturbed, a pointy bra humanized with
two babies' heads, a foot in the mouth of a balaclava,
or a surplus of stiff wig hair ill-contained in the crotch
of a man's Y-fronts. A puerile amusement, I agree, but
the job itself made no demands on our mental faculties.
With summer, the most delicious and longed-for time
of year, deadened for seemingly terminal stretches of the
day, playtime helped.

We wouldn't have gotten away with our dumb she-
nanigans, I suppose, if our employer, Mr. Scully, hadn't
been so distracted by Mary Smith, a university student
from Southern Ontario staying with her aunt for the
summer while she worked at the store. Mary didn't need
a name less generic because she was staggeringly beautiful. In the looks department, movie star material. This
intrusion of loveliness might have driven the two of us
wild with envy—you could hear male necks snapping
whenever she walked by—except that she was of the
Sapphic persuasion. No one in our town knew what to
do with this information, let alone how to spell it. What
was involved? We had no manual. Lezzie, gay? For
many, that such improbable preferences existed beyond

rumour, the National Ballet, and the Catholic priest-hood, simply didn't wash. Calling the druggist a panty-waist was about as far as it went. Hence, a captive of disbelief and misplaced desire, our boss kept his beady, albeit dazzled, eyes on Mary, while the two youngest members of his staff goofed off and dicked around as required by our needs.

Toward the end of the day, starvation imminent, I helped myself to a second sugar doughnut from Mrs. Inch's shopping bag while she wriggled and squirmed in the dressing room trying on a swimsuit several sizes too small. The grunting and muttering and sighing was not unexpected—I'd heard it all before—but the scream she let out caught me by surprise. She whipped back the dressing room curtain, stared at me in alarm, snatched the doughnut out of my mouth, grabbed her shopping bag, and fled, her dress unzipped and her shoelaces flapping loose.

*Huh.* Either the winter weight she'd packed on had been more disconcerting than expected or she'd sprained her wrist trying on the suit. I peeked in. The black swimsuit lay on the dressing room floor like a shucked husk from a cannibal's picnic. Other than that I couldn't see anything else that might have caused her snack-snatching distress. No perky plaster lips nor any other dismembered bit of mannikin anatomy had found its way into the dressing room. No timorous beastie from the order Rodentia. My guess, she'd suddenly remembered the pot of stew left simmering on the burner at home, or realized in a blinding flash that her son, Norman, had not only knocked-up his sister but was also the culprit siphoning gas from the family car.

"What was all that about?" Bea slid in beside me and poked her head into the dressing room.

"Norman."

"Ah. That shit heel. Say, I forgot to mention. Your dad came in looking for you. You've got a sugar mustache, you know."

"What?" I grabbed a man's psychedelic-patterned shirt off the rack and wiped my lip. "When?"

"Before lunch." She stared down at the swimsuit. "Wouldn't be caught dead in that."

"Why didn't you tell me?" I hadn't filled Bea in on my sorry situation. Too weird even for me.

"No big deal, is it?"

"Did he say anything?"

"Too busy ogling Mary. Why, what's up?"

"Oh… the usual." Tearing up minimally, I quickly hid my face in the shirt and blew my nose, adding an element of earthy realism to the phantasmagoric material. The hanger clunked against my chest. "Parents."

"Tell me about it."

After work, who should meet me at the door with open arms and copious apologies for stress and suffering endured but… no one. NO ONE. No caresses, loving or otherwise, no heaping plate of food, which even a *lowly* flea-ridden mutt might reasonably expect after an emotionally taxing day. I didn't think my mother would show. Doubtless, she was a goner, murdered by my father (and who could blame him), which is why he'd come to see me at the store before skipping the country or killing himself. No wonder he hadn't left a message with Bea, the phrasing on this one definitely tricky. But *damn*, I'd have to hoof it to the morgue if I wanted to see them at all, say my last goodbyes and *thanks* for nothing, eh. Did we have a morgue in town? I pictured some dank, chill, formaldehyde-redolent room in the hospital's basement, my parents forever becalmed and fully married (finally!) on their respective slabs, holding hands (death grip), their last few nickels covering their eyes (beavers up), while our furniture, stacked in the corner, awaited the underworld movers.

Instead, I decided to go to Neath's Hotel up the street and treat myself to dinner.

Maxine set down my plate of fries and gravy with uncharacteristic delicacy, positioning it with care before me. Normally, the plate hit the table with a velocity that sent the cutlery flying in all directions.

"Hmph," she said. "Terrible what happened to your parents."

"Yeah." I tried very hard not to put this in the interrogative, too ashamed at this advanced stage in the misadventure to admit to ignorance. *Everyone* but me had to know.

"Some people," she added, with a brisk snort.

I nodded solemnly, this being a statement you couldn't very well disagree with.

She gave my shoulder a supportive pat, then sailed off, soon getting back into Olympic form in delivering a plate of liver and onions to Father Shea. He ducked.

So what *had* happened? Obviously, it wasn't good. On the up side, Maxine hadn't said, "Honey, your folks are at peace now. It's for the best." Or, "They're in a better place." (Well, that wouldn't be hard, would it?) And the cops hadn't come looking for the next of kin or a crazed, blood-spattered juvenile delinquent. Maybe 'some people' had totally ripped them off, yet naked and penniless they could have come to the store for some underwear. I do get a 10% discount.

I paused then in my investigative reflections to appreciate the beauty of the meal before me, the grease glistening magically under the hotel's florescent lighting, knowing that if my supper's nutritional constituents were questionable, my high-achieving liver would meet the challenge. Also knowing, unhappily, that there'd be no more gravy for me. There goes my future, I thought. I'd have to marry for money. Quickly. Really quickly, as I didn't have a cent on me. Payday wasn't till Friday, and I'd forgotten to dip into the petty cash at work, as occasionally happens during lean times. I immediately got going on the fries before anyone— some people, for example—decided to snatch them out of my mouth.

After I'd scraped the last delectable glob of gravy from the plate and licked my fork until it gleamed, I pushed back the chair, and signalling to Maxine at the cash, said, with as much *savoir-faire* as I could muster, "Put it on my tab, will you?"

"Sure thing, hon," she called back.

Hey!

Heading out I found that, while much restored, I had no idea what to do or where to go. I needed refuge for the night, but, coincidentally (a 'real coinkydink', as Uncle Earl would say), all the bearable members of my extended family happened to be away. My grandmother, Albertha Pinkham, had gone off on a cultural tour of North Bay and Timmins, while my Auntie Viv and Uncle Clyde were in Vegas (only to return a week later ten dollars to the good, several pounds heavier, eyes widened by spectacle—including a Sammy Davis Junior sighting—and disenchanted forever with our backwater). As for the rest of my relations? Although my parents, unforgivably, had ditched me, I didn't want to expose them, or myself, to the family's exfoliating commentary, nor to the torment of bad TV. Bea's place was also out of the question. Whenever her parents saw me coming, barbed wire of a psychic construction sprang up to defend their cozy enclave from invasion.

I wandered down to the dock, thinking to stare moodily into the water as I pondered my fate. Dark night of the soul. Although, in fact, it was Daylight Saving Time, so not a problem. I had enough light, actual and innate, to get by just fine. The problem, as it turned out, was the unsavoury human element also attracted to the town docks. In my adolescent innocence, it simply didn't occur to me that with my abundant physical charms on display and reeking of pheromones, the Patchouli of the natural world, this might be an injudicious thing to do. Outside of our own homegrown creeps, there were plenty of strangers hanging around the dock in the summer, including tourists and sailors off the freighters that hauled coal. Drifting along, wistful and aimless, I must have looked like easy pickins.

But nothing is as it seems, yes?

Passing by the public washrooms, I acquired an admirer who'd been leaning up against the side wall, hard to see at first because he was colour co-ordinated with the stained cement block. I walked on, he followed. I walked faster, he picked up the pace. Unwisely, I'd headed for the unpopulated end of the dock, past the fancier crafts, to where only a cluster of motor boats and a tug were tied up and battened down for the night. If I hadn't attracted the notice of my new friend, I might have considered taking one of the boats out for a ride, or bedding down in the tug.

The situation required some quick thinking, luckily a specialty of mine.

Here's what I planned to do. I'd turn and give him the evil eye, sizing him up, knowing he'd be rank with adjectives: oily and beaky, with tiny eyes, broken teeth, hairy ears, scabbed lips, and a skewed rat-tail that stuck out stiffly from his misshapen head like a clawed back-scratcher.

He'd utter a crudely vile overture, his lower lip sticking to a wonky canine.

This would make me want to shriek with delight, but instead, in no mood (long day) to be wooed by a steaming pile of do-do, I'd enquire, primly, "You think so?" And, possibly inspired by the store mannikin game, would add, "Don't see how you're going to manage that, pal. With your dick stuck up your nose."

Then, during the brief interval in which he reaches up reflexively to check this surprising anatomical arrangement, I'd take my leave. Fast.

Thus prepared, I turn and clap my eyes on an utterly gorgeous boy, some mysterious transformation having evidently occurred. Long-limbed, curly blonde hair, tanned, full lips (no scabs) shaped into a winning smile. Does Mary Smith have a brother? Mary, whom we'd taken to calling The Virgin Mary Smith given her gloss of impenetrability, her celestial remove. To be sure, despite her avowed orientation, she seemed a different order of being, untouchable. Her heavenly counter-part, on the other hand, appeared to be more willing to engage with the descendant of a hominid.

He says, softly, "How about it?"

"It?"

"It."

Such a dinky word 'it', downright *itsy*, a mere toy, lexically speaking. But… hey! why not! *ohhhkay* wonder boy, let's unpack that baby and see what's in *it*. Let's be *it*, do *it*, fly *it* high!

He takes a step closer. I gaze into his marvellous eyes and see… strange to say, something slither away, something dark and quick that's gone into hiding some-where in his ocular recesses. Nothing as material as an eyelash. Which reminds me, before leaving work, Mary had mentioned a meeting, or some such, up at the hotel bar. She said it with a wink, and I had assumed she was teasing me, inviting me to play along with what I increasingly took to be her suitor-repelling ruse.

Mr. Beautiful places his hands lightly on my shoul-ders and presses down with an equally light, yet firm, touch. My knees buckle slightly.

"It?" I say, as comprehension dawns. "It!" A word now so pointed with indignation that, if possible, I'd stab him with it. Speech begins to boil in my chest like heartburn. Words, none of them appreciative, rush into my mouth, but that wretched "it" acts as a kind of plug, and I repeat "it" again. A couple of times, trying to spit "it" out.

He frowns and gives me a troubled look, perhaps wondering if he's encountered a mono-verbal idiot, the stammering town fool. (We do have a few of those.) Readily enough, his expression shifts into a craftier mode, for who in his right mind is going to come to the assistance of someone gibbering a personal pronoun?

Right, so, what did the girlfriend of *Homo erectus* do when words failed her? She grunted, I suppose, and tried to grow a bigger brain. I didn't have time for that. Instead, I stomped on my man's sandal-clad foot (*he* grunted), and, turning tail, appropriately enough, took off. I pelted down the dock, past the public washrooms—where the original threat *still* loitered—and up the hill, hustling straight back to the Hotel.

I had a date! What Mary had said to me after work, purposely misleading or not, had finally sunk in.

As I crossed the street, my cousin Nile cruised by in his black Buick. I gave him the finger. He gave me the finger. We laughed. Communication at its finest.

Entering the lobby, I turned toward the bar opposite the restaurant where I'd been earlier. Ladies and Escorts. No lady, no escort, and underage, but in dire need of a drink, I pushed through the heavy doors and through the haze of smoke that met me, wending my way around the tables until I found them in a corner, blockaded behind an array of empty beer glasses and pissed to the gills. Clearly, they'd had less trouble getting these glasses to their lips than the coffee cups that morning.

"There you are," my mother said. "We were beginning to wonder."

"Nice of you." I sat, crossed my arms, and glared.

"Hungry, sweetheart?" My father rose, a tad unsteadily, and listed toward the bar.

A bag of peanuts for my trouble. Great. My glare powered-up a megawatt. "I was almost molested!"

"Were you, dear?"

Dream come true for her, I'm sure. "Have you guys been here *all* day?"

"Practically. We live here now."

"What?"

"Upstairs. We rented some rooms. Cheap, too. There's a hotplate and everything."

"We already have a whole house rented, remember? With a *stove*."

"We got kicked out. The mayor. You know what he's like."

I nodded, getting interested. The house on the hill belonged to him.

"He's always had his eye on me."

"Gross."

"Not that I'd ever, you know—"

No comment.

"Anyway, *something* snapped. He came by after you left for work and told us to get out. Gave us to the end of the week. If you can imagine!" She seized her glass and knocked back a last swallow of foam.

"So you left this morning instead?"

"We showed *him*." She slapped the glass down.

"Sure did."

"Don't know how we managed it, Hero. But, you know, it was kind of fun. Nile helped. We threw all our stuff in the truck, stored it in Albertha's barn. I'm sure she won't mind. I mean, she will, but *enh*... here we are!" Mother made an expansive gesture in celebration of the ambience. "Our new home."

I looked around, noting several features: the disabled chairs, the burns on the floor, the ashtray cornucopias of stubbed-out butts, the signed Tommy Hunter photo nailed to the wall and curling at the edges, the nub of fossilized barf stuck to our table, the gathering of pie-eyed and hee-hawing—or quietly weeping—members of this dismal club.

"When I'm a lawyer I'll *sue* the pants off him."

"Good girl." She patted my knee. "Not to worry. I'm sure he'll be dead by then."

"Ladies," my father said, sweeping in with a tray of drinks.

Before me, with a flourish, he set down a Shirley Temple, topped with a twee, pink paper umbrella. Of all humiliating things that had happened to me that day, this had to be the worst. How old was I? Eight? I didn't even get the bag of nuts. Admittedly, matters improved after I took my first aggrieved sip. The Shirley had matured considerably, having been spiked generously with vodka. I glanced over at Phil the bartender and he gave me a friendly nod. Very gratifying to receive some respect not generated exclusively by myself for a change. The drink, and the one to follow, soothed all of my major organs, unhealthily rattled by the day's trials and tribs. And, later that night, while I didn't exactly tap dance up the stairs on my way to bed, "The Good Ship Lollipop" eased my passage all the same.

My room looked out over the back parking lot. Having already tested the hotplate, thumbed through the Gideons Bible, and checked the mattress for creepy-crawlies, I stood for a long time at the window, hugging the thin hotel pillow to my chest and taking in the view. I watched as they emerged from behind the bushes, the storage shed, the garbage cans, shadow-swift in their tens, then hundreds, wave upon wave.

Charcoal-furred, barbed tails, horns.

# In Other Words

For a time I performed my inquisitional duties publicly, the better to get my hands on the goods. I had established my office in the restaurant of Neath's Hotel at the table nearest the kitchen where the staff sat when they had a moment to grab a smoke or flip through a movie mag or consider the placemats. This prestigious spot I'd secured via a slow and steady infiltration. During the weeks that my family remained homeless, we took up residence at Neath's downtown, which gave me my first in. Once I'd absorbed the weirdness of our new arrangement and mastered the art of lighting a cigarette on my room's single functioning hotplate burner without setting fire to my hair, I began hanging around the rest of the joint, making myself useful as opportunities arose. For Beth, the switchboard operator, I fetched Cokes and ham sandwiches from the kitchen, listened at length to her domestic woes, and filled in for her when she needed to retreat to the ladies' room (which was a *lot*). Research heaven. As Victor, the dishwasher, liked to say—with much less cause—*I know what I know.* You bet. After enough forays into the kitchen ("Onions!

165

No fucking *onions!* Excuse my French, dear, but could you run down to. . . ?"), I was in like a dirty shirt. (And all too frequently wearing it, my mother being notably lax in the clothing care department.) In due course my school texts began to appear on the staff table, marking my spot and handily dog-earring my squatter's rights when required to be elsewhere. Before long, elsewhere began calling to me less and less.

High school, basically a petting zoo, had squat to offer someone who was keeping her eye, rather than her hands, on the local fauna. Everyone passed through the restaurant at some point, their crimes, no matter how mild or rank, intact—hence the ideal lookout for a round of moral winkle-picking. The coffee may have been ghastly, but the fries were hot, and the view even better.

One day, Vic noticed me observing a table of Hydro guys who were snickering slyly amongst themselves— the subject a female, no doubt—and felt moved to offer me advice.

"Hero, there's something I have to tell you."

"Yeah?"

"Men."

"Uh-huh?"

"Don't trust what they say. They're after one thing and one thing only."

I gave this utterance some thought.

"You mean like a tool? A drill, say? Or a Thompson screwdriver?" I was a big fan of the hardware store.

"Well, yeah, I wouldn't mind a decent drill myself, but that's not what I, uh—" Blushing ensues.

I was delighted to discover that I at least looked innocent. "So this 'one thing' applies to you too, Vic?"

"No, of course *not.*"

"My dad?"

"Geez, Hero. Morland? He's a nice man. So what if he did kill that—"

"A rumour, Vic, remember that. How about Doc McIvor?" He happened to be seated at the front of the restaurant, endangering his own health by digging into yesterday's 'clam' chowder.

"Gosh, no. A doctor would never—"

*Au contraire* (excuse my French). Our good doctor had been after 'one thing' of mine and got it. My tonsils. My first intimate experience with a man and I'd been out cold the whole time. I sometimes wonder what he did with them. It's disconcerting to lose bits of yourself.

"What about Nile?" My cousin had the reputation of being a ladies' man.

"Nile?" A look passed over Vic's face that would have befitted a timorous faun catching sight of Pan, rock star of the hedonistic woodlands. "Uh, Nile doesn't need to—"

"Never mind. I know, I *know.*"

"And I know what *I* know. Don't forget what I said."

So there we sat, steeped in knowledge, although none the wiser about what the Hydro guys were saying. And it should be noted that while men remained something of a mystery to me, I was far savvier about the ways of the world than dear, sweet, walleyed Victor. You couldn't live in a hotel, slowly navigating the hallways and attending to the racket humans made when they got together in a depressing room with a bed centre stage and nothing else to do, without knowing what was what. On top of that I had access to a wide range of educational reading material, including Beth's copy of *Peyton Place*, the expired men's magazines sourced from the garbage cans behind the drugstore, and the Bible in my night table so helpfully provided free of charge by the Gideon Society and in which one might encounter an inordinate amount of begatting.

For all I knew the Hydro guys might have been sniggering about Vic himself, no he-man with his messed-up eyes and clubfoot. He'd been gamely serving tables, helping Maxine get through the lunch crowd, and when he lurched into action, the lads could barely contain themselves. Bad enough a male doing women's work, but a physically damaged one at that. A joke in slo-halting-mo.

"Tip?" I asked, although not requesting further advice, as Vic blundered past later carrying the guys' dirty plates. Grim-faced, he pushed through the swing doors into the kitchen.

"Pigs." Maxine landed in her chair at the table with a laden plate of spaghetti.

I don't agree with disparaging animals, but let it go. "No tip?"

"Condom."

She menaced a meatball with her fork, harrying it around her plate. Good thing those guys weren't from here and not likely to show again. Maxine had a wicked serving arm and a style that brought decapitation-by-crockery to mind.

"Vic tells me that men only want one thing."

"Sweetheart, I could of told you *that*."

"But it's not true, is it? It's got to be more complicated, they've got to be. What about Einstein?"

"He's dead."

"Uhh, right. What about… the Pope?"

"He's fixed."

"He *is?* Wait, not that—"

"Look Hero, it's true, true and *true*. I oughta know, dear. Don't think you won't find out yourself, either. Just you wait."

Yet wasn't that precisely what I was after, the truth, the whole truth, and nothing but?

"*Man*, Letty's a lousy cook." Maxine pushed her plate away, retrieved her smokes and lighter from her apron pocket, lit up. I loved watching her—the languid draw, the smoke curling out of her nostrils, the delicate ash at the tip of the cigarette growing longer and longer—suspense!—until finally, before it tumbled off and shattered, she flicked it smartly onto her plate of spaghetti.

"No obits today?"

She shook her head. "Not in the mood."

Maxine had this pastime which kept her agreeably occupied during her breaks and from which I'd learned a thing or two about euphemism, a linguistic device that formed a rind of respectability over many a juicy situation best given an airing. Flipping her receipt book open to the back, chuckling, and often humming Frank Sinatra's version of "Fly Me to the Moon," Maxine composed obituaries for those customers unfortunate enough to catch her eye—or ire. For some reason—okay, I *asked*, didn't I—she shared these with me, although not with the others. This is how I learned that the mayor was a 'powerful negotiator' (bully), the druggist a 'confirmed bachelor' (homo), the United Church minister's wife 'utterly carefree' (off her rocker), and that Beth's husband, while 'convivial' (a drunk), had recently become a 'marital enthusiast' (bigamist). After a while you got the hang of it, language embedded in language: swordsman, working girl, free spirit. Following this formula, my immediate family, if wiped out, would at best, and most kindly, be summed up by the phrase 'of no fixed address.'

While evasive obituary code amused her, Maxine dished out her designated deaths in a more straightforward manner, with none of this 'passed away' or 'met his maker' business. *She* was the maker in this reckoning and, like one of the Fates, an extremely efficient one— no holding back in the detailed dispensation of car crashes, house fires, heart attacks, stabbings (one with a fork), drownings. Sobering to think that the one taking your order and chatting you up might also be sizing you up for a bespoke wooden suit.

Harmless fun all in all, but it no doubt encouraged this tendency I had toward investigative activity. What less generous souls might call, oh, I don't know… prying, snooping, sticking my nose in other people's business. Be that as it may, I did like to get to the bottom of things, although the particular one I got to during my time in the hotel was vexingly dark.

What's newsworthy? Violence, scandal, celebrity, sex—preferably all in one big grotty package. Not much in that line happened in our town outside of the heated goings-on at euchre parties or in the dance hall. Likewise, not much of lurid interest transpired in our only hotel. Hardly notable were the everyday comings and goings of salesmen, tourists, curlers attending bonspiels, hockey players snowed-in, government functionaries checking up on us. There might be the occasional girls' night out, or stag, or quaint tryst among the married-to-others, or the odd male slipping like a shadow down a certain hallway to visit a certain woman.

If you care to know, the certain woman occupied Room 29 on the second floor and was registered under the name of M. Jezebel—so either in possession of a sense of humour, or taking advantage of the free Bible, same as me. Regarding the humour, I never heard her laugh while I hung out in the vicinity, although I'm aware that some people keep their amusement to themselves. Also, in her line of work conceivably not a good idea, a fit of laughter during an awkward or fumbled transaction. I'd say it's a safe bet that this is not the one thing a man wants.

What bothered me at first, outside of the fact that no one seemed to care about what happened to her, was the other fact that I, the unofficial house detective, did not once lay eyes on the woman—alive or dead. During the brief period that her fate retained titillating value, everyone I interviewed claimed to have seen her and their descriptions all varied, taking full advantage of having a deceased stranger to work with. One would describe her as being busty and bouncy—"Watched her comin' down the stairs, whooee!"—while another countered with, "Not enough meat on them bones." One swore her to be a flaming redhead, another a bottle blonde. Short, tall, too young for the business, or too old. The only thing everyone seemed to agree upon was the manner of her death. Died suddenly, which is to say, by her own hand. I didn't buy any of it.

"Real pretty, yeah," said Vic, going on to describe someone I *had* seen plenty. "Leaving by the back way with this guy, not sure who he—"

"Sounds more like Hero's mother." Maxine took a long drag, squinched up her eyes, and gave me a shrewd look.

"Hey... you know, I think it might've been your mum, Hero. Huh. But who was that guy she—"

"Vic, go get us a coffee, will you."

"Sure thing, Maxine."

Once he'd obediently shambled off, I let out the usual resigned sigh in order to clear the air and get the investigation back on track. I wondered if Maxine had been nursing any theories of her own. "You going to write an obit for this poor woman?"

"What'd be the point of that? She's dead." Maxine, having switched to roll-your-owns, spit a shred of tobacco off her tongue, a direct hit on the ketchup bottle. "And don't you be feeling sorry for her, some dumb broad. Hooking? Drugs? Got what she deserved."

The sigh I let out now was not resigned. I'd get on with it, despite this attitude generally held. Slow going all the same. Having asked more than a few probing questions, what had I netted so far other than unwanted advice, suspect intelligence, and a raffle ticket (Glee Club)? Oh, and I'd been propositioned. To protect the innocent, I won't disclose the name of the culprit, but the exchange went like this:

"Hey, cutie pie."

"Excuse me."

"Want to [unspeakably lewd suggestion]."

"*Excuse* me."

"C'mon, you know the score."

"Aren't you married?"

"In a manner of speaking. . . ."

Well, fly me to the moon. Actually I did better than that. I flew upstairs (passing Paul VI on the way, a frisky rodent clenched in his maw) to talk to Selina, the room cleaner who'd found the body. Traumatized by the discovery, she'd been off work for several days to recover (and do a little shopping), but was back. I knew I had to speak with her before her story became contaminated by too much exposure or started to shapeshift into an entirely fantastical other.

"Not a stitch on!"

A good start. "What else? Lots of blood?"

"No blood, Hero. Everything nice and tidy, no puke or nuthin', the bed all made up. Would've been real easy to clean, that room, if she hadn't, you know—"

"Yeah, for sure. What about the drugs? Pill bottles toppled over on the night table? Booze? Bottles on the floor?"

"Nope, not a thing. Glass of water, that's it."

"What'd she look like, Selina?"

"Ordinary girl, nuthin' special. In her twenties most like."

This corroborated what I suspected. Although I hadn't laid eyes on the victim, I had, one evening while filling in for Beth on the switchboard, heard her voice. A young voice, soft, familiar, like the voice of a friend or a sister. I could almost feel her warm breath filling my ear. She asked for a local number and I explained that first I had to connect to the central switchboard in town and make the request. Rose, a friend of my Auntie Viv's, by chance working the night shift, *had* to cross-examine me first, asking why I'd been cutting so many classes lately (talk about nosy!), and I said that I'd been sick, and she said that I shouldn't have let them take my tonsils out, and I agreed with that, then *quickly* asked if she could *please* put this call through for a guest at the hotel. Rose made the connection and we all listened, expectantly, our mutual breaths mingling in this magic moment of modern communication, while the line at the other end rang and rang. No cigar. M. Jezebel hung up quietly, without a word to either of us, and likely spoke no further words to anyone for what remained of her life.

"One funny thing—"

"Go on."

"Her hand."

"What about it?"

"Looked hurt, sorta twisted. Like this." And here Selina demonstrated, getting down on the floor of the hallway, stretching out on her side, doing her best to look dead—mouth slightly open, tongue poking out—and scrunched her left hand into an awkward position, as though it had been cruelly wrenched.

Lord love a duck! I had the clue I'd been searching for.

Only the day before, puzzling over one of my textbooks, Vic asked me about my studying Latin, what use could it possibly be? The simple answer to this was that I had no choice—at our high school you took what you got, our teachers only hazarding the northern boonies out of desperation, bravery, or cluelessness. But who wants to give a simple answer? *Ergo* I explained to

Vic—*Victor*, yes?—the advantages of having a second language, if one spoken only in Hades. (Admittedly, my Latin homework was so serially borrowed that by the time I handed it in, it practically constituted another language altogether, unrecognizable to anyone.) I further explained that my future legal practice required it.

"Some bossy know-it-all opponent gets up my nose and it's '*Ipso facto*, fatso! *Ipsissima verba!*'"

"You calling him a sissy or you telling him to piss off?"

"Both. More or less."

"Neat."

Neater, though, was the use to which I intended to apply my knowledge of the language. Or I should say, my knowledge of some of the translations I stumbled upon while sidetracked from the mind-numbing labour of mastering declensions. Ovid, I discovered, was my man and *Metamorphosis* my book. It blew the Bible clean away. When Selina told me about M. Jezebel's hand, I thought about the story of Procris and Cephalus, and I thought about it because I'd seen a painting of the former while flipping through an art book in the town library. Let other juveniles giggle over nudity in *The National Geographic*; I took in far more sophisticated sources, once enjoying in the earlier pages of said art book the depiction on an antique vase of a man balancing a wine cup on his penis. Had anyone in town managed to pull off this trick during any of the drinking parties out in the bush? With a bottle of Labatt's 50 or IPA? Can't honestly say, as I'd never been invited. But I doubt it!

So let me introduce Cephalus, a guy with a magic spear (yup) *and* a dick in his name. And what does he do with his spear but kill his wife with it. By accident, although given that she'd been spying on him, what did she expect? Not death I'm thinking, but there you go. He weeps and moans while she dies in his arms, happy apparently, their bond having been re-confirmed as she slips off to the underworld. A good story in Ovid's telling (if not in mine, sorry), but a bit of a head-scratcher. As is the painting of the slain Procris, which I now had an urgent need to examine again.

Braving the dragon, Miss Brothers, a.k.a. Smothers, in her lair, I cautiously pushed open the door of the former jail that served as the town library. A cool, green, cave-like sanctuary, vigilantly guarded.

"Why aren't you in school?" Smothers enquires, testily, my foot barely toeing the threshold. She's seated at the front desk, light flashing off her cat's-eye glasses.

"Er, it's a spare."

"What do you want?"

"Um… a book." Yeah baby, a book! Is that too much to ask for??

"Don't say 'um.' What book?"

"An art book." Or rather, *the* art book. How many does one town need?

"Why?"

"For a project I'm doing?"

"Our high school doesn't teach art."

Tell me about it. "It's for Latin class. I'm writing an essay on Ovid."

"His name is not pronounced Oh-vid. Not like *O*valtine. It's Aw-vid."

"Right." Like saying ahhh for the doctor, I guess, but defend those tonsils. "Aww-vid."

My hazing over, Smothers pulled the book out from under the desk and walked it over to the table in the centre of the room, set it down, and, curiously enough, opened it to the page I wanted, a half-page colour plate of Piero di Cosimo's *A Satyr Mourning over a Nymph*.

"You can't check this out," she said, meaning the book itself I assumed, because I had every intention of checking out the picture should she snap the volume shut on my unblemished and blameless hand, pressing it like a flower between the pages. I nodded, moved over to the table, and got to work, while she resumed her seat at the front desk, and watched me, gimlet-eyed, not even pretending to do otherwise. Just waiting for me to improve the artwork with flourishes of my own? A mustache or two?

Never fear, I found this painting to be almost unbearably beautiful as is. Cephalus doesn't appear in it, although a young satyr does, grieving for Procris. There's a dog, also mourning, that resembles Ruby who lives on a farm outside of town, a river in the background (more dogs, birds), and delicate flowers growing in the grassy area surrounding the body. The satyr, who has one hand tenderly placed on Procris' shoulder, utterly defies your lustful satyr stereotype. Gentle, compassionate, handsome (definitely dishy, and sufficiently hairy, no mustache needed). Strange as it might sound, he reminded me of Vic, but with a much cooler do, goat's ears, and hooves instead of a clubfoot.

Procris, lying on her side, is wearing a pair of gorgeous sandals, toenails painted, and is only partially clothed. Her breasts, 34A, are exposed. (Her cup does not "runneth over," as my father is given to observing

of the less well-endowed. And while on the subject, I
have to say that there was no want of exposed knockers
in the art book. The artists responsible being mostly
male, I had begun to wonder if the one thing men
*really* want is a full-blown set of their own.) Although
Ovid wrote that the spear pierced her in the breast, in
the painting the wound is in her neck, and it's fresh,
blood spurting out. But it's the positioning of her left
hand that most interested me. It's oddly crooked in the
very same way that Selina demonstrated during her
death-mime of M. Jezebel. I knew I was onto something, but what?

So absorbed was I in pondering this question, that
I practically jumped out of my skin when Smothers,
standing directly behind me, spoke.

"No accident, Hero."

"No?"

"Look more closely." And here our efficient and
resourceful librarian produced a magnifying glass of
Holmesian proportions and zeroed in on the other
hand. The dead woman's right arm was tucked under
her body, but the hand lay open, the palm visible,
unlike the left hand.

"It's all scratched up."

"Slashed," Smothers corrected. "This young woman
had been trying to defend herself from an attack. Knife,
spear."

"Is that why her left hand's bent back like that? It's
broken?"

"Nerve damage." She moved the magnifying glass to
the neck wound. "Her throat's been cut, the cervical
cord severed. This makes the wrist flex and the hand

curl up like that. You see how your eye is drawn to it by the satyr's hand on her shoulder. It's as clear as an arrow pointing to the cause of death.

"Murder."

"Murder," echoed Smothers.

One does not expect justice to be carried out in the Greco-Roman mythological world (one is not a total nit), but in ours? Let's just say, that no matter how determinedly I made my case, no one would listen. Not even Selina, who, ever adept at sweeping dirt under the carpet, soon swept the details of her discovery in Room 29 under a proverbial one. And then the carpet itself disappeared. In this, I understood the hotel's owner, Mr. Neath (powerful negotiator) to be involved.

"For Crissakes, Hero." Maxine studied her pointy nails, the scarlet flipside of her yellow fingertips. "You're smart, we all know that. But get real, will you. This isn't some TV show."

"Yeah, Hero," Vic chipped in. "Like Ed Sullivan… you know."

Vic said this so wistfully that I didn't hold it against him. But my patience was thinning.

"Look, I'm not spinning plates on sticks here."

"That's not what I'm saying, kiddo."

"And that's not what *I'm* saying, *Maxine*."

Agreed, I wasn't Perry Mason, but not even Raymond Burr was Perry Mason. Last resort, I plunked myself down beside Doc McIvor, who was about to endure a bowl of chili, and asked his opinion.

"Waiter's Tip," he said.

"Pardon?"

"Also called Erb's palsy. It affects the hand in that way. The fingers curl up like a waiter taking a back-handed tip. Some people have it from birth, nerves damaged during a difficult delivery. That unfortunate woman may have had the condition from day one."

"But not necessarily?"

"The coroner wouldn't have overlooked anything suspicious. Bruising on the neck—"

The Doc's attention had been diverted by the ketchup bottle, which he picked and frowningly examined as if *he'd* discovered the vital clue to a mystery. It only proved, however, that hygiene in the restaurant was abysmal, and I could have told him that.

"But the coroner is, um [don't say um], convivial."

He set the bottle down and looked at me. "True. He's a genial sort."

"No, I mean he's a drunk, half-cut most of the time *and* half-blind, plus he's got a thing for corpses."

He didn't respond right away, perhaps contemplating whether or not to laugh, or wondering whether he'd damaged my mental faculties while removing my tonsils. "Hero, he said quietly, "someone's been filling your head with malicious nonsense."

"But Doc, don't you think it's fishy? Her death? A woman born with a hand like that wouldn't *be* a... uhh, working girl like her. Don't you need at min two functioning hands? Manual labour, isn't it? Like being a carpenter, or a—" In a rush of inspiration, I had been about to say 'prick layer,' but bit my tongue.

"Not to put it too bluntly, my dear. A disabled hand of this nature might have been a benefit." He looked down into his rapidly cooling bowl of chili, regretfully. "Some people, men, have unusual… requirements."

A doctor, he'd seen it all, I suppose. And now he saw even more.

"Um, hold on. Hero? Are these kidney beans *moving*?"

If I'd accomplished little else in this whole affair, if M. Jezebel had kept her own counsel about grievous harm suffered in death as in life, I at least had the satisfaction of saving a great many of my fellow citizens from a bacterial takedown. Not that I got any credit for it. On the contrary, after everyone witnessed me nodding enthusiastically as I peered into Doc McIvor's lively bowl of chili, I got pegged as a whistle-blower. The restaurant closed 'indefinitely' while the health department dealt with the wildlife. (Maxine, when she heard, dealt with it in her accustomed way, kicking a mouse clear across the dining room.) Mr. Neath informed my parents, his voice much louder than necessary, that they were to vacate their room at the hotel PDQ and to "take that mouthy little minx" with them. My mother, increasingly troubled after the death in Room 29, had been agitating to leave in any case. If she knew anything about M. Jezebel's end, she too kept her own counsel.

I missed the hotel, but our new place on the waterfront, an airy (i.e. derelict) hyphen between the marina and the dry cleaners, was also biologically vital. After a surprising incident which occurred on our very first night in residence, we took to calling it The Reptile House. What happened was this: mid-dinner (bacon and eggs served on the family pattern paper plates), my father, mouth crammed full, abruptly stopped chewing, his gaze pop-eyed and fixed on the wall behind me. For a minute, I thought that a Heimlich might be in order—I'd once seen Vic perform this nifty maneuver, none too successfully, I'm afraid—but when I turned to look, saw a water snake laboriously wending its way *up*. Up the wall!

"Oh, for heaven's sake," my mother said, dropping her plastic knife.

She pushed her chair back, got up, walked over to the snake, plucked it off the wall, and with it writhing in her hand, strode outside to the front porch and hurled it high into the air, where it hung, buoyed by astonishment. Briefly. Before anything large and winged swept in to nab it, before it achieved the status of an omen, the snake dropped into the lake, gathered its wits, and swam away.

I should mention, too, that I won a gardening trowel with that raffle ticket. An exceedingly nice one—stainless steel, oak handle, genuine leather toggle looped through the end. Whether or not the draw had been rigged, and the trowel had been awarded to me as a taunt or as an encouragement to keep on digging, digging, didn't exercise me in the least, for I had every intention of doing exactly that.

## Too Bad

"Ruby," I said to the dog on the farm up the road, "I'm taking my love to town."

"Oh, Hero," Ruby responded with a heart-rending whine. "Don't! Don't take your love to town."

"Done that yourself, Ruby?"

"Done it, Hero. Sad, *sad* to say."

Excellent advice, Grade A, but I kept on. What else was I to do with this entanglement in my chest, this weight in my vitals? At some point in the past several days I seem to have swallowed the contents of someone's chaotic sewing basket full of sodden clumps of felt and open safety pins. Had to haul it somewhere, had to walk it off in momentum-generating protest. Yet the more dust devils I raised on the fried August road as I stomped along, the more indignant were the demons that danced in my head.

I'm sure my friend Beatrice would have found my pilgrimage funny if she still resided in a place where humour pertained. My *former* friend. We'd had a few incendiary words. It started with the shoes, rapidly spread to the dresses, and from there to the groom himself. All hideous—*someone* had to point this out. Sparks flew in the service of truth, and, before you could invoke the volunteer fire department and feature them grappling fumble-fingered with their suspenders, years of friendship had been wiped out, reduced to a burned-hair stench and the charred recollections of more amicable times.

Thus had I fallen from my esteemed position in the wedding party to a disgraced and outcast Maid of Dishonour. Not only that, but I had to be the only one in town, with the possible exception of Ruby, not invited to the wedding. So, you know, I thought I'd just go anyway and add my spectral dust-enrobed presence to the festivities.

Walking, taking my sweet time, enjoying the scenery. (No choice, unless I could find a horse and learn how to ride it.) I had on the contentious bridesmaid dress, a thrombotic number more suitable for a centenarian, screamingly synthetic and snapping with static. The clot-coloured and fashion-defiant heels I'd left at home in a sick bag where they belonged. Bea, ever thrifty, must have been planning to save us the sartorial expense of all future occasions, including death. Plus she'd look halfway decent by comparison—for once, despite being pigeon-toed and overweight, bulging out of a dress also an eye-gouging, bargain-basement special. It's possible that I made select, unedited remarks of this nature to her.

So here I am hoofing it up the road barefoot, risking cuts, stubbed toes, and hookworm, but not, as you might suspect, in a penitential frame of mind. The real wound, the one inflicted on the muscular organ still thumping gamely in my chest, required the salve of an apology, or, failing that, universal recognition that I'd been hard done by, snubbed, grossly insulted, kicked when down, purposely misunderstood, undervalued, and *egregiously* ditched for a substandard male, a pro-to-cheater and wife-beater. If Bea thought she was striking out on the road to matrimonial bliss, I'm afraid she was suffering from a brain-eating delusion. An issue I fully intended to air during the service when Reverend Cowley asked if there were any impediments to this union. Impediments! Friends and neighbours, have a seat, kick off your own shoes, unstopper those concealed mickeys, this is going to take a while!

You get to know a patch of road. I'd lived on this one off and on over the years, long enough to stake a claim. While my parents played musical domiciles—and whatever else they played at—moving, always moving, I learned not to put my feet up, not to get overly attached to the ever-changing interiors. The contents of the outdoors they at least couldn't hurl into a box in a fit of dissatisfaction and lug off to some more temporarily pleasing spot. From where we were located now, in a rental perilously close to identifying as a trailer, a two-mile hike would get me to town, or in the opposite direction, to the Dump. Destinations of equal interest and both offering entertainment along the way.

Dumpward lay an elderly apple tree in which I could sit and pitch rotting fruit at the passing traffic—at the postman, Mr. Pock, on his run (he waved), at the Wilson's or Petty's returning from a shopping trip in town (they waved). Shrubs swathed in tent caterpillar nests held considerable fascination, reminding me as they did of the gauzy veils women once wore while out motoring in their Model-T's, the contents of the veils now a busy squirming mass of wormy life. (Rather like that presently collecting in the church for Bea's wedding.) Once Mr. Pock had made his deliveries, there were mailboxes to check, find out who might be hearing from whom, hands both familiar and strange to parse, copperplate or barely legible. At times I've hovered at the foot of a long lane—the house at the end entirely obscured by the foliage of ancient oaks—a blue envelope balanced delicately on my palm, wondering, wondering... overcome by this excess of secrecy.

Ditches in either direction held treasures, but mostly if you were ten years old and considered shards of smashed brake lights or discarded empties worthy of note. No longer ten, indeed tragically close to one-score and senescence, I found that recently, despite the lure of the Dump itself (you never knew what you'd find!), the road to town beckoned more. Beckoned, while at the same time encouraging a brisker and less observant passage.

Be that as it may, I'd never lost my appreciation for the old comforting sights along the way, always stopping, for example, to pay my respects to the Bathtub Madonna who presided in her porcelain grotto in the Minelli's front yard. Despite her reliably placid demeanor, the Virgin could have used more respect, too, for I noted again today that no one had bothered to clean the bathtub ring before installing her, which gave her a subfusc nimbus composed of sloughed Minelli matter, cells and pubes (from the evidence a furry lot), and God knows what else. Also, since my last visit she'd developed a skin problem. A scum of algae had begun to spread across her face, giving her a greenish, alien aspect. Nor was her complexion improved any by that bullet hole in her head. Some yahoo out joyriding and sick of peppering road signs had plugged her right in the noggin, causing her some mental ventilation. Or... some kid with a BB gun or a 22? Or, more likely yet, a shot gone wild, our boys hardly what you'd call sharp-shooters. Dunno, this was me trying to be reasonable, a strain at the best of times. Sad, though, if intentional, very sad. We girls were going to have to stick together.

"Bitch!" Bea had shrieked.

"Whore!" I'd countered.

"Hag!"

"Douche!"

I'm afraid we got into it, slapping down insults as though caught up in a particularly nasty game of Snap. I *may* have called her a "butt hole" at one point, which I should say, in case it's not obvious, embodied an attempt to move away from those tiresome, female-spe-cific deprecations. Neutral ground—an anus is an anus is an anus. Doubtful that my efforts were appreciated.

I nodded sagely to Mary before moving on and wished her, if not a speedy Assumption, then at least a well-deserved divine intervention.

Next stop, the mystery house. Not that I stopped, no one did. In a car, you speeded up when you came to it, gazing straight ahead. Walking or biking, you held your breath until safely past. The house itself didn't appear to be especially dreadful, certainly no worse than what most of the town or countryfolk lived in. Not your classic haunted house—decayed, creaky-hinged, bat-infested, lapped in darkness. Not by any means. What we had here was a compact one storey, white clapboard, bevelled living room window, no curtains, cement steps leading up to the side door. Yet I'd never heard the house named, as most people's places were— the Murphy's, the Kidd's. (Even, in many cases, if the families no longer lived there. Even if the house no longer existed.) This place never came up in conversation. So what had happened in there to earn it this eerie silent treatment? I don't know. Lips were firmly sealed on the subject and could not be pried open. Nor were the gasbags, who normally had a robust appetite for lurid detail, any more forthcoming.

My theory is that the house contains the signature of evil, its mark, no more legible than a grease spot on the kitchen table. Unreadable yes, but a deadly contaminant if even tangentially parsed. Touched in whatever way—with recollection or speculation—this sick sigil will be activated, sending out waves of depravity that will drift invisibly into our lives and… gut us.

Containment. That described the communal project, didn't it? Like building a new arena. Only this one was more of a holding facility for a certain breed of knowledge having to do with the very worst that human beings can do to one another. Have to own that I was itching to ferret out what that might be. I gave the place a surreptitious scrutiny in passing, half tempted to go over and take a good look through the bevelled— bedevilled?—living room window. But then, *holy moly*, I did sense a chill, a sensation of some ghoulish force reaching out to me, trying to draw me in, and I stepped up the pace, hastily recollecting my mission in town.

Little did I know that something equally uncanny was heading my way.

I *did* hear it coming, saw clouds of dust roiling in the distance, causing me to skitter aside. Shortly after, very shortly, a black car peeled past, skidded to a stop, pulled a U-ey, then rumbled up beside me. My cousin Nile, our local Lothario. He rolled down his window, looked me over.

"Nice dress," he said.

"For a stiff."

"Shoes?"

I shrugged. As our communicative style didn't allow for a surfeit of information, I didn't bother referencing my level of sophistication vis-à-vis crap vinyl pumps.

"Hop in."

Hang on, did I hear that right?

**Q:** How long had I been waiting for this very invitation?

**A:** All my life.

No, not quite all. There were stretches during pre-puberty when I couldn't stand the guy, my too-cool cousin. And then, and then… one day I noticed something about him. I'm not sure what it was, but he had it, he'd banked it, and he wasn't giving it away. I developed a crush that felt exactly like that, as if I'd been dropped into a compactor, and my brain, which would have been very useful in this situation, extruded like paste out of my ears. Packaged for romance, I was ready to roll, while yet the squarest of girls. It wasn't only me, either. He had lineups longer than the one for *The Shaggy Dog* that played for a weekend at the Legion years ago in my more heedless days. Indeed, Nile couldn't pass by a bed of flowers without the whole clump blowing their pollen, hurling it wantonly in his path.

That was then. Now, with my grey matter restored and regenerated, I planned to put it to much better use. University in the fall, career, success, wealth, acclaim, that sort of thing. Not for me, throwing it all away for some handsome hick. Let Bea reap the rewards of small-town, small-minded life, trapped forever in a claustrophobic house with a corral of tiny tots and Small Balls himself hollering for the little woman while he swills his small beer and blows the ass-end out of his smalls—

"Something funny?"

"Nope."

"Get in."

"No thanks."

"Suit yourself."

"I will."

Couldn't help but crane my neck to peer around him into the dark interior of the Buick, though. Over the years it had acquired many imagined features and as a consequence possessed an almost mythological allure. My mother had always warned me about getting into the car with Nile. Strictly *verboten*. I often wondered if she'd spent time in it herself during her more experimental days, feeling free to do the relevant research seeing as her own reputation was already shot. Front seat, back seat, a much younger man, hot stuff.

I took in the purple plush seat covers, the plastic hula-girl figurine on the dashboard, and the staggering number of souvenir blue garters looped over the rearview mirror. (Nile exercising an updated *droit de seigneur?*) I observed what I could, closely but dispassionately, like a forensics specialist at a crime scene. And then... I promptly walked around to the passenger side, pulled open the door, and got in. Somehow Nile seemed to know I would, for he'd kept the car idling, hands draped over the steering wheel, staring straight ahead, waiting. Now he gunned it, the car backfired, and we were off, leaving nothing behind but a hail of gravel spinning through the air.

I settled in easily—and gratefully enough after the long walk—wiggling cutely as I rooted myself in the cushy plush seat and began to appreciate the over-all ambiance. I found it like being in a chapel, softly lit and soothing, hushed despite the purring engine, otherworldly... although noticeably deodorized. For a moment I couldn't place the smell, definitely not of your usual fake-pine air freshener. This had more of a drugstore familiarity. Bea and I had often liberally sampled the smelly stuff at Crawford's, dabbing every nook and cranny of exposed flesh until we reeled through the door reeking. And laughing, and snorting, merrily. (Not that I cared to think about that.)

Brut! Unmistakably Brut. The source of this killer cologne could only be Nile.

I turned to him, surprised—he being more of a nat-ural-odour man—and finally, fully, took in the spectacle of him tricked out in dress shoes, black pants, and a clean white shirt, black tie stuffed in the pocket. A suit coat had been tossed onto the back seat. He appeared to be going to a whole lot more trouble than a wedding not his own warranted. And even then—

"What's the deal?"

"Best man."

"No, you're not."

"Pinch-hitter."

"What happened to Stretch?"

"Fishing."

"What about Squirt?"

"Dehorning the cattle."

"Milton?"

"Broken leg."

Okay, we all have our priorities, but I was beginning to suspect that this defection from the wedding party had more to do with the speechifying required of the best man at the reception. I could see how having to knock more than a few words together that didn't involve baseball or imbibing stats might be a terrifying prospect for these guys. Either that or the powder blue tuxes that Bea had shipped in at great expense had sent them scrambling.

"Bea'll be steamed."

"She's already steamed." Significant sideways glance from the cousin here.

"How'd she talk *you* into it?"

"Her big day. Why ruin it."

"So where's your sucky blue suit?"

Now I get a full filleting look from Mr. Goody-Two-Shoes and further conversation is nipped in the bud.

We drove on in thoughtful silence—me anyway—and soon arrived at the church. Lots of people were milling around in their finery, chatting, laughing, shooting the breeze, primed for a good time. Some were climbing the stairs, eager to get a good seat, the bride's side or the groom's, either would do, no one takes this division too seriously. Besides, who isn't related to both of them somewhere along the line?

Nile and I gazed in passing at the hearse parked in the prime spot in front of the church gate. This particular vehicle might seem prematurely placed at a wedding if one didn't understand our practical arrangements here. The hearse was as close as we came to having a limo service, and, the Grim Reaper being only an occasional visitor, our funeral director, Glanville Goodwin, felt it would be a waste not to give his vehicle a more upbeat function and himself some extra income. Any morbid or unlucky associations the meat-wagon may have brought with it were charmingly lightened by the colourful crepe paper pompoms with which it had been gayly decorated.

Nile cruised along. Parking was tight, so he drove around the block. We gazed at the hearse again. He drove around the block again. A space opened up—no doubt a guest rushing home to retrieve the forgotten wedding present, the toaster or the waffle iron (those perennial domestic anchors)—and he sailed right past. Third time around the block, he stopped, idling in mid-street, parallel to the church gate.

"Want out?"

"Not really."

He drove on and I got to thinking about what he'd said. Did I want to ruin Bea's 'big day' that badly? Me alone? The big day that precedes a lifetime of small days to follow? The loose threads in my chest tightened painfully, as if they'd been given a good hard tug, keeping their burden in place. I began to picture Bea's big day as the mouth of a cave, yawning hugely. She enters and begins walking. At first it's fun—there's cave art! stalagmites! diamonds glittering in the walls!—she's enjoying herself. But before long

193

the passage gets narrower and narrower, and she has to start crawling on her hands and knees, getting slimed with bat shit and shredding her wedding dress. The dark deepens, and deepens, there's no way out, she gets stuck. Desperate, she calls out to her *very* best friend, who happens to be a high-powered divorce lawyer living in swish digs in Toronto (or someplace classier). *Hero, Hero, I'm stuck!*

"Too bad," I say.

"Yeah, rough rocks."

Whoops. I hadn't meant to speak out loud. I gather that Nile's referring to the wedding, which we appear to be leaving far behind. Main Street, past the hotel, up the hill, down the road that leads out of town, across the bridge. . . .

"*Yeah*, suck eggs sister... um, where are we going?"

"Splitsville."

"More specifically?"

Nile shrugs. "Down south? We'll check out your new school."

"I'm not going *now.*"

"Why not?"

"It's hundreds of miles away!"

"So?"

"My parents will kill me."

"Nah." Then he adds, mysteriously and somewhat alarmingly, "You and me, baby."

*Oh, Christ*, he's abducting me. Or perhaps we're eloping. I could get married too, of course. A revenge not only served cold, but served like fast food. Quick, cheap, and very bad for one's health.

What *would* my parents say? If they noticed. They had become preoccupied of late—with one another of all things, newly enamoured. I'd sensed that there'd been sexual activity on the premises. If there was a romantic *je ne sais quoi* about the most recent squat box that we'd washed up in, I for one had missed it. Not so very long ago my mother had clasped my hands in hers and regarded me with maternal concern, although I suspect her main concern had more to do with getting me out of the house.

"Hero, I'm worried about you," she said. "All you do is study. You'll wear out your eyes if you keep this up. Are you having any fun, at all? A boyfriend? Surely there's someone."

So, basically, she was worried that I wasn't getting knocked-up in the usual fecund rural tradition, while I, regarding her with equal concern, worried that she *had* been knocked-up. Wasn't it a bit late for this? Some sibling filler for the upcoming empty nest? I knew that I'd been a disappointment, that for me she envisioned no life of illicit extramarital affairs, no hot nights fumbling with zippers under scratchy bushes lit with fireflies. Sad, in her view, that all I had to look forward to was financial security, success in my chosen field (and not the field out back of the War Memorial), honours, prestige. While other girls were out catching their man, I'd be pursuing my calling, which lay in catching criminals. I glanced over at Nile. Two birds with one stone?

Nothing for it, I propped my dusty feet against the glove compartment, wrapped my arms around my knees, and settled into our escapade. I told Nile all about my plans for school, the courses I'd be taking, and how, as a lawyer, I'd be bringing scum to justice. Or I'd bring justice to scum, depending on the circumstances.

I explained how arson investigations work, fingerprint-ing, and blood splatter analysis.

"Handy," he said, nodding.

I talked about my parents and his and our various relatives, books read over the summer, the stranger I'd be sharing a room with at the residence and how I hoped we'd be friends and not drive each other nuts, and offered him a miscellany of views on this and that, until finally he laughed and said, "Hero, shut up. You talk too much."

Funny, but Bea had said the same thing, point-blank and without the laugh.

Would I? Didn't they know that the uninvited guest at my christening had handed me an outsized crate of words as her gift and said, "Use it!" And to the best of my ability, I had, and would.

On we went, on and on, Nile driving, me mono-loguing, each in our element. After a while I switched on the radio to a C&W station and we sang along to the sorry laments, pouring our all into them, a little taken aback by our conviction. At one point Nile stopped the car and got out to shore up the muffler with his tie. I had a short nap and woke with his suit coat tucked around me. The farther south we travelled, the more the horizon opened up before us, wider and brighter, and I don't believe I'd ever been happier. Although, I have to confess, that's one thing I left unsaid.

# Acknowledgements

A number of these stories have appeared in various literary magazines, including *The Malahat Review, The New Quarterly,* and *The Walrus.* Some subsequently resurfaced in *The Journey Prize Anthology, Canadian Notes & Queries,* and *Best Canadian Stories.* "Bigmouth" first appeared in a handsome series of Biblioasis limited editions.

The medical information cited in the story "In Other Words" with regard to Piero di Cosimo's *The Death of Procris,* may be found in an article in *The Guardian* ("The fine art of medical diagnosis"), concerning the teaching and sleuthing methods of British surgeon and art critic Michael Baum.

*Merci bien* to the Ontario Arts Council's Writers' Reserve program.

Terry Griggs is the author of *Quickening*, which was nominated for a Governor General's Award, *The Lusty Man, Rogues' Wedding*, shortlisted for the Roger's Writer's Trust Fiction Prize, and *Thought You Were Dead*. Her popular children's novels include the Cat's Eye Corner series, and, most recently, *Nieve* (Biblioasis). In 2003, Terry Griggs was awarded the Marian Engel Award in recognition of a distinguished body of work, and in 2010 honoured with the installation of a Project Bookmark Canada plaque in Owen Sound. She lives in Stratford, Ontario.